Spacing Out

By

Creative Writing Students of
La Quinta High School

La Quinta High School
Westminster, California

Spacing Out

Edited and Compiled by: Amanda LaPera
Senior Copy Editors: Kelly Ho, Nancy Huynh
Copy Editors: Bethanie Luu, Phuong Traceyle, Jacqueline Truong
Senior Section Editor: Vivian Tang
Section Editors: Diane Bui, Kayla Nguyen, Aysha Pena, Kathy Pham, Krista Phanpraphou, Sophia Trejo
Design Editors: Jennifer Ho, Tiffany Le
Cover Designed by: Jennifer Ho, Tiffany Le
Interior Editors: Hiep Do, Ngoc Pham

Published by La Quinta High School Creative Writing Class

Dedicated to the dreamers

Table of Contents

MY FATHER'S SHOES

by Hiep Do

I found an old pair of derby shoes
Lying in the corner of the garage
The gray of dust has contaminated
Their once untainted black color.
The laces dangle aimlessly
With no one to tie them
For the past ten years.

I remember every morning
The derby tapping
Against the hard wooden floor
As my father headed for the door
Without giving me a kiss
Or saying goodbye
His sacrifices went by in silence.

I put the derby shoes onto my feet
The cold of the morning dews that lingers
from the daily routine of the past decades
still has not left the derby, not one bit.
The shoes are heavy, chaining me to the ground
But I still lift my feet with pride
And take the very first giant step.

EPIPHANY

by Vivian Tang

Isn't it crazy how time has passed?
From the pains of yesterday to the comforts of today
How everything seemed too soon to end
But was only the beginning of something new

Forcing myself to always look down
For the ground to open Heaven's gates
Waving at the silence murmuring into my ears
Like the friend who has long been gone

Such a beautiful feeling
Of wonder and answer
I finally understood the reason
For love and happiness

They both begin with *me*.

SCOLIOSIS

by Nancy Huynh

Tilted to the left
  Can't stand upright
    Back pains at seventeen
      No sleep at night.
        Braces during puberty—
          But not for the smile—
            Always on my back
              Kept me mobile.
                Occurred during growth
                  But now disrupts my height
                    I swear I'm five feet tall,
                      If you straighten out my spine.
                        I may be out of place
                          But please realize
                            How can I get life straight
                              If I'm leaning to the side?

HIROSHIMA

by Bethanie Luu

The sand and dust
Blow in my face.
I stumble through
What used to be
My home.

The grass
Greener than before,
Still carries
The scent of death,
And the buildings
Are shadows
Of my
Once beautiful
Hometown.

And as I approach
What once was
The playground
Where I would always
Frolic about,

I am hit
With a wave
Of painful memories
As I recall
The bomb,
Plunging from the sky
Like a fallen god.

The people
Screaming
As they ran.
I remember a hand
Pulling me away
As I simply stood
And watched
As the bomb
Erased everything
From the earth.

It was such
A beautiful sight
Until Death
And Destruction
Overcame us all.

A PRECIOUS GEM, A PEARL

by Ngoc Pham

Unnoticed by her surroundings
She is caught off guard
By a person capturing her image,
She halts halfway

Her eyelids heavy
Her thoughts run erratic
She stares at the man in front of her
What is he doing?

They stay in the same position
He notices the shine near her ear
A glimmer that makes him realize
It is a gem, A precious gem, a pearl
It may have cost thousands, if not millions
Something of such worth could only be worn
By this fine lady in front of him

A precious gem, a pearl
The man admires her beauty
Her pale features encapsulated the gem's beauty
Along with her posture, the way she stands proud

But the more he looks at it
The more he realizes it isn't real

A fraud, a fake, no longer precious, no longer a pearl
Now a shiny questionable item
He asks her about the gem
Of what name it may be

16

She chuckles at his question
This was no precious pearl
It was synthetic
With a name she knew not of

He gave a dejected sigh
But continued to talk to her
Silence no longer between the two
As they slowly become closer.

COMPUNCTIOUS

by Kelly Ho

This blood that covers my hands
Red bindings that only I can see
The tears that bleed from your eyes
The reason I am locked in this paradise

A moment I unknowingly
Watch as you fall to the ground
With knives so unwittingly spoken
Tied to this world though you're gone

Your eyes once beautiful glass beads
Now cracked and destroyed
Because of the winter storm
My imperfect self ruins your beauty

Moments once beautiful now stained
Our hands once held must part
Before your cracks break you to pieces
My suffering in exchange for what I've taken

I'll pay for my sins with my life
Your summer warmth shall never reach me
I'll let you go with a smile
Knowing I've saved you from myself

Don't hide your tears any longer
I'll tell you words I don't believe
And watch your tears swell one last time
Be free while I remain in this misery

DESKTOP

by Jennifer Ho

I didn't want to delete it
It was always there
In one neat folder.
It seemed like it belonged
Seemed.
I dragged it to the trash bin
And closed my eyes
Farewell,
To the virus;
To the love that can never be restored again.

LOVE

I am scared of confessing
Not wanting to ruin what we already have
But where will I store my chaotic feelings?

Bleeding out of my heart?
In a glass jar, where it'll burst into red shards?
Or in a secret journal, where it'll rip the pages into shreds?

Instead, I keep my undeniable love for you hidden
Like the sun behind a blanket of gray clouds
Hoping one day it will finally get to shine through.

A, B, C Love is Not Easy

by Sophia Trejo

Absolutely horrible is what love is,
Believe me, it's not as neat as it looks.
Corrupting not only the heart, but the brain as well.

Determined to not to lose my mind over him always falls short,
Every thought is consumed by him and I don't know how to stop it.
Failure is what I am faced with.

Get a grip and see that it's no use.
Head for a different direction, maybe?
Invest in a new hobby?
Just forget it, that won't work either.

Keep thinking about those past memories,
Longing to see him again.
Missing those moments when it seemed real
No, it was all a lie.

Of course it was.
Probably should have seen it coming but blinded by love.

Quit it already!
Rip him out of your mind,
Shut him out of your thoughts,
Think about something new.

Unexplainable feelings,
Vast emotions that I can't express.
Waking me up at night, never getting enough sleep.

Explain this to me because I don't get it.
You had this all planned, didn't you?
Zealous over my emotions.

GHOST WORD

by Christine Vu

WORDS CAN HAVE THEIR own story. Yet, their stories are not well known. In this dictionary universe, word entries are sentient, personified. Their creators, the editor-gods, drew up a human, with ink flowing in their veins, and breathed life into them. These humans, the words, can speak and move about their world. Words grow as they get used or developed more often, similar to human development. Do not mistake them for humans, no matter how much they appear like us. Not while ink flows in their veins rather than blood. Not while their lifespan coincides with the duration of dictionary publications. Like anything alive, the words can age. Papers yellow and crinkle as the ink fades away. Woe to the few who go beyond that state.

THE SUN POKED OUT of the clouds that were already drifting away, despite the lack of a breeze. The sunrays reached down to the many buildings arranged next to each other in the plaza below. These buildings were assigned a specific label, each one reading the name of a language. Different languages gathered here for their day, to meet with their friends or other languages, to gather news, or perhaps prepare for a party.

Although all of the buildings had an open-air courtyard in the middle, each one differed from the other. One may have a fountain, a flower or greenery garden, a tree centering a grass field, or perhaps a statue.

Each building contained many distinct rooms, their doors located either inside the building interior or outside facing the courtyard. One room could be the sustenance supply room, while the room next door could be a crafts room.

The most populated building was the English language building. Many other languages were curious of what occurred inside.

Around the door of the English Words meeting room, one of the busiest rooms in the English language building, the Italian words huddled around, hoping to pry the door open as discreetly as possible. Some of them peeked through the open window blinds, between each yellowed vinyl slat, their hands pressed against the glass.

"Why is everybody here so excited?" the Italian word Morte asked a friend, Sbaglio, who shrugged before ambling away from the glass window. Morte followed Sbaglio into the halls, allowing the other Italian words to try to peek through.

"I did hear talk about something new," Sbaglio said, "but I can't translate what they're saying."

Morte nodded and was about to respond when somebody within their Italian group rose above the crowd. "Quick, leave. Somebody's coming to the door," that word urged.

At the sound of approaching footsteps, everybody scrambled away from the hall. Not a word lingered around a corner for a glance at the door.

The word Dictionary opened the meeting room door and searched around the hall from left to right with furrowed brows. "I'm sure I heard something," Dictionary muttered before closing the door.

"What is it?" the word Future asked. Dictionary shrugged. Future scoffed at this response. "It's the other languages snooping on us again. Perhaps somebody should teach them a lesson on how to stop being so nosy."

Dictionary turned towards Future. "Well, you don't snoop in on their meetings, because you already know everything. Everybody else snoops in on meetings because they're not psychic like you."

Future huffed and turned away with crossed arms.

The word Welcome rang the brass bell at the front of the room to gather everybody's attention and waited for the noise to die down before sauntering over to a cardinal red backdoor. "Everybody, meet the new word." Welcome opened the door.

All of the English words moved around pushing to the front or standing on chairs to catch the first glimpse of the new word.

A small figure revealed from the shadows with paper white skin, almost blinding in the lights, and contrasting ink-black hair, choppy and chin-length. The word's name printed across the baby blue shirt in a typewriter font.

When catching everybody's gazes, the new word averted eye contact and took a step towards the wall.

Whispers flew from everybody's lips. 'What is that word?'

The new word lingered by the wall while Welcome placed a hand on Dord's shoulder. "What is your name?" Welcome asked.

The new word looked down at its shirt and played with the hem. "My name is Dord."

"And what does that mean?" Welcome nudged Dord forward.

"Um, it means density."

"Oh?" a voice exclaimed from the right side of the crowd. Everybody turned towards the source. "I'm Density." Density had sand colored skin and loose charcoal hair, an obvious sign of age. Folks there grew darker with age while their hair faded like ink. "Maybe we're related. What sort of density?"

Everybody turned their heads back to Dord.

Dord fidgeted before replying, "the physics and chemistry kind."

Some of the words turned to the words Physics and Chemistry. Chemistry shrugged, waving away the attention. This happened way too often.

With a scrunched face, Physics said, "I've never heard of a Dord in my field."

Somebody laughed. "Because Dord is new, silly."

Density wrapped an arm around Dord's shoulders. "Since we're pretty much the same, I'll protect you from these folks." Density smiled. Laughter and exclaims of "Hey, excuse me?" filled the room. Density turned back to Dord, and added, "If you ever need me, I got your back."

Dord cracked a tiny smile.

Like smoke, whispers suspend in the air, never to be waved away. This was recurrent, but the content was far from mundane. Rumors of a misprint in the dictionary traveled about, even beyond one language group. The almighty editor-gods, the words' life-giver and creators, could kill somebody with the final clicks of the typewriter. Or at least Future foretold so. Nobody could confirm who the word was but that didn't stop everyone from pointing fingers.

When passing by, Dord was aware of the others stealing glances and felt the weight of their stares. Although Dord didn't want to admit it, the reason was clear: perhaps Dord was the misprint, despite the denials. Without knowing what to do or what to believe Dord brushed off their gossip.

The next day, the sun shone brighter than usual. With harsher sunlight come darker shadows. It was difficult to see through the dark shadows and glare of the sun.

"Haven't you heard?" somebody asked a word in a hushed voice. "Someone's not supposed to be here."

"Who do you think it is?"

"I bet it's the new word. The two snuck glances at the new word and smirked at each other. They trotted over, one of them rubbing hands together. "Hey, you."

Dord looked over, seeing two taller words drawing closer, although it took a while for Dord's eyes to adjust to the bright sun. Their skin was many tones darker than Dord's, hair and eyes many shades lighter. These words were evidently older. They wore the same clothes as the English words. Dord read the names on their shirts, Palace and Ostracize.

"You're the new kid, huh?" Palace asked.

While nodding, Dord's body stiffened, shoulders hunched, instinctively aware that these words shouldn't be trusted.

"So your name's Dord? That's so weird. Where do you come from?" Ostracize asked.

Dord's mouth opened then closed. Dord was unable to answer.

"Newbie doesn't know," Palace said to Ostracize with an elbow bump. The two laughed disdainfully as one of them pushed Dord aside.

Dord staggered, but regained footing. "I—"

"I bet this word isn't even English," Palace heckled. This made the two double over in more laughter.

"Can you stop that?" Dord asked with a straightened back.

Ostracize and Palace snapped their heads at Dord with a hardened gaze. They stepped closer and in a low tone, Palace asked, "Do you know who we are?"

"We're part of the Etymology Elites. You've heard of us?" Ostracize said. Dord nodded. "You know what we do with the likes of you?" Dord gulped, not wanting to hear the rest. Ostracize raised a fist. "Here's what we do."

Dord huddled on the ground with holding head and upper body, and peeked through folded arms to see the attackers' next move.

Palace and Ostracize smirked at Dord's quivering form. They closed in on the little word.

"Tell me, what are you?" Palace jabbed.

"You don't even have history," Ostracize said.

Eyes squeezed shut, hands covering the neck, Dord tightened up, waiting for another incoming beating from the two. Dord counted the seconds to note for the next time. One… Two… Three… Four…

A recognizable voice called out, "Leave Dord alone, will you?"

Palace and Ostracize turned around towards the source and stepped back.

Density strode over to them and maintained eye contact while placing hands on hips and firm footing. "Is something the matter?" Density asked.

"Newbie here doesn't have history," Palace sneered with a curt nod at Dord.

Density gave a backward glance at Dord, wide-eyed but no longer quivering. Density faced Palace again. "So what?" Density said. "Nobody has history when they first arrive."

"Your little friend here lacks an etymology," Ostracize said.

"I'm sorry to tell your snooty, nescient self, but not everybody has an etymology as rich as yours." Density gave an eye roll. "Surely, you must know about the words: Conundrum and Big and Squirm and Yank and Malarkey and—"

"Alright then, Density. Fine, we get it," Ostracize said.

Ostracize and Palace huffed away.

Density smiled while pulling Dord up. "That wasn't so bad, huh? You're fine."

Dord stared at the ground. "They were so sure."

"Who? Those two?"

"No, everybody. Everybody believes I'm the misprint."

"Don't worry. It'll pass." Density patted Dord on the shoulder before walking off.

There was something heavy in that shoulder pat and Dord noticed.

ONE DAY THE FOLLOWING week, the weather was cooler than the usual sunny days. Clouds as thin as dandelions covered the sky with the sun only partially visible. Most words were outside taking an afternoon break.

Dord tugged on Physics' sleeve for the millionth time. Physics, lying down, sighed and rolled over to Dord with a dull gaze.

"Just tell me, do you know who I am?" Dord asked.

Physics glared and turned away.

Dord frowned then tapped Dictionary on the shoulder. "Can you tell me about dord?"

Dictionary tsked and waved the question away.

Dord's lips quivered. Arms waving to grab their attention, Dord approached Chemistry and Future. "Can you explain to me about words in the dictionary?"

Chemistry twitched. "Did you hear that?"

"No," Future said, "I didn't hear anything."

Dord's breathing hitched. "Must I speak louder? All I'm asking—"

"There it is again. What's that?" Future wore a blank stare.

"Let's go somewhere else where we can't be bothered," Chemistry said as the two departed.

Dord's head drooped and lips quivered, arms slowly sliding up to cover the upper body. Dord leaned against the nearest wall, sliding down into a curled form with eyes lifted upward.

Footsteps approached.

Dord straightened up, smiling upon the sight of Density. "Hello there."

"Hello Dord," Density greeted, voice strained. The sun created shadows over Density's face.

"Density, you told me you'll help me when I need it. Can you tell me who I am?"

"I am so sorry, Dord. I can't help you anymore."

Dord's head shook. "No, please don't do this. You can't say I am…"

"On your own." Density's head dropped, hiding a swallow. "I wish you luck."

With head slumped, Dord trembled. Never had the word felt so separate from the world, a discarded leaf no longer accepted by the tree community. A gust of wind blew past the word. Goodbye leaf.

Dord jumped up and bolted to the center of the quad. "Does anybody here recognize me?" Arms outstretched, Dord wailed.

No response, just the wind blowing by.

There was faint scribbling heard from the heavens above. Everybody diverted their attention to it. They knew. The misprint would be fixed and there would be a new dictionary printing.

Dord mouthed out a "No." The word whisked out of the quad and into the nearest building opening, escaping everybody. Bolting down the hall then around a corner, another hall then another corner, and kept at this until the building revealed its dead end.

Dord halted in front of a restroom, panting, then shouldered the stuck door enough to open a smidge. The word slipped inside and fumbled for a light switch. The flicking yellow lights revealed cracked tile walls and floors, colors indistinguishable, and vandalized stalls and mirrors. Toilet paper and odd rubbish littered the water stained floor. Dord's nose crinkled at the mess. The word tiptoed over the mess to the cleanest wall possible and stumbled to a corner, one arm up to land on the wall. Dord panted, head tilting back to the ceiling.

Why?

Dord raised a fist pounded against the tiles.

Why?

Knees bent and legs descended to the floor.

Why?

Dord curled into the corner, weeping and rocking rhythmically.

Not many words know how it feels to die, and some will never know. Those who do know can't explain it once they've experienced it.

Dord wasn't alone. There appeared a plastic horse about a reach away and muffled footsteps further outside the door. Dord decided the horse shall be a friend, even if they've only met. Dord smiled sadly, leaning against the horse, fingers curling around its smooth body. The Dord's dim eyes closed.

Welcome rings the brass bell to catch all of the others' attention. The English words are having a meeting.

The Italian words, no matter how hard they pressed their ears against the door, couldn't understand what was being discussed.

Sbaglio and Morte watch the other Italian words. They scoff. It was just another boring meeting, no reason to snoop. Then the lights flickered.

Morte's eyes glanced at the commotion through the window.

"There's a new printing," Sbaglio commented.

Morte nodded then sighed. "I suppose my English friend will be busy tonight."

The English word Death paced on the other side of the mahogany door. Death pulled out a pocket watch with an hourglass dangling from it. Without anyone noticing, Death opened the door and slipped away from the meeting.

"We have a new member to our club."

"For the last time, Foupe, this is not a club," Kime said. "This is hell, you can't leave this place."

Something caught their attention. A horse with Death at the reigns entered into the room. That was how it's always been, Death bringing in another misprint.

"Dord," Death said with a hand to the second word sliding off.

"Another one," somebody commented.

Dord scanned the room in confusion.

"Kid, you're dead. You're in another world," Kime said.

Dord whirled back to the other words. "What now? Another world?"

"So what's your misprint story?" Foupe asked with a smile. "Some writer misread Soupe and wrote me down."

"I was a typographical error," Kime added.

Dord faced away from them. "I don't know. Maybe something like that."

Foupe shrugged before leaving. "Take your time." Kime followed after.

Dord replayed what Foupe and Kime said, over and over again. "This is it? I'm now a ghost word."

Certain words do not realize they are misprints until it's too late. By the time a word does learn of its fate, nothing can be done. Once gone from the dictionary, the words become ghosts.

Few ghost words exist. The editor-gods dare not repeat mistakes.

RISE AND FALL, RINSE AND REPEAT

by Kathy Pham

Once he was a beggar
A fool, a grain of dust
Unable to differentiate
Between whom to trust

A fool he may be,
But he rose to the top
Like a hawk taking lift
To the skies up above

He soared, as he gained
Riches and fame
His heart, it grew black
Having been lost to the flames

His mansion, a great luxury
Burnt to the ground
For his partner once loyal
Favored the crown

Oh sorrow, oh pity
They say he was wise
But he trusted a snake
And thus he died

But dead he was not
A beggar he'd become
Reliving the life
He had once left lonesome

"I will get my crown back
I will get my revenge
I will not let him be
Until I see him amend"

Wisdom he had gained
Experiences he used to live
The man unsheathed this blade
Invisible to all
He shall not yield

Jumping the ranks
He became mighty once more
He met his former ally
The same as he recalled

His enemy had spoken
"I hold you no grudge
We are on the same footing
I ask for peace
For fighting would become nothing"

"I agree, it is so"
The man, he replied
"But I have not forgotten
The treachery you hide"

"Then what do you want
My money, my jewels
I'll give you anything
For I am not a fool"

The man, he responded
His tone gentle and smooth
"I have set this mansion on fire
Now the two of us shall duel."

WHEN I WAS LITTLE

by Daniela Solano

when I was little,
I dreamt about living in a cottage in the woods.
waking up in the morning
to kill breakfast,
pick berries in a bush that's
conveniently placed outside my small home.
I dreamt about shopping at farmers' markets
and writing poetry in a flowery meadow
as I watched the sky turn purple.

I wanted to live a dream.

however, something tragic happened.
the world turned upside down with the realization
of what a real youth is made of.
these sweet dreams of peace and serenity
mixed with poetry and meadows,
morphed into dreams of parties, puffs of smoke
loud music, slick guys, spiked drinks, and destruction.

I miss the days of simplicity,
and seeing the world with bright colors.
now I sit on the rooftop,
and watch everything crumble before me.
everything I was working for,
all deteriorating in front of my
very eyes.

LOST IN LOVE

by Christina Nguyen

Blinded Heart

They had been close friends for a short while,
She felt lost; how could she love someone else
when she couldn't love herself?
Not realizing all she needed
was already in her mind.
But, she kept pushing the truth away.

Before the Love

She had enjoyed her life being single,
Able to do anything without someone
 telling her what's right or wrong,
I miss those carefree days.
All that precious time I lost,
There was no commitment,
no forced submission.
I don't need love at all.
Yet, She couldn't help but grow new feelings.

Fragments of her heart

Her mind conflicted and heart split,
She didn't know what she wanted anymore.
She felt torn, unsure if she truly was ready
 for a new relationship.
Her heart was already divided,
But she could never get rid of that piece of her heart,

She fiercely opposed the thought,
Falling into despair.

Déjà vu

She had felt like this before, this déjà vu.
Both surprised and not, she was left lonely again.
She had never been bothered
by the company of loneliness before,
So why did she keep trying to push it away?
I don't need love at all, I just don't,
She swore to herself.

Memories

She rummaged through old cardboard boxes,
Getting ready to move into a college dorm.
A year had passed.
It feels like it was just yesterday
She dug through her belongings
She found her scrapbook.
flipped through the pages.
There she was, holding puppies tightly to her face.
I miss them.
On the next page,
smiling brightly, wearing a summer dress at a beach.
That sun blinded me,
She continued through her memories, until...
She reached the last picture
 she and her ex, before their breakup.
She was smiling and extending her arm towards him,
Yet, she peered into her eyes;
they showed a hint of sadness.

Saying Goodbye to Love

It was a mistake;
I shouldn't have fallen in love with him.
She closed the scrapbook,
No. I'm done with love.
She left the book behind, packed her boxes.
Dimming rays of sunlight faded from her bedroom window.

She looked around one last time,
the scrapbook on her couch.

All of her memories had been stored
 in that small, tattered book.
It feels like I'm letting a piece of me die.
She couldn't bring herself to leave that book behind.
But… it's for the best.
The sunset turned plum purple,
inviting more shadows into her room.
…goodbye.

The Man in the Mask

by Aimee Geck

I FIRST HEARD ABOUT the Maskman when I was five.

"If you don't be good and finish your dinner, the bogeyman will come and take you away from us," my parents would say.

In retrospect, that was one of the most terrifying things you could've told a five-year-old. A strange man will kidnap you and take you away from all your friends and family just because you aren't behaving. Parents say crazy things to make their children do what they want, And it works.

Now I tell my children the same story. My daughter bolts from the room when I tell the story, but my son comes running and jumps onto my lap. He even wants to meet him.

"Daddy! Daddy! What does he look like?"

Here's the thing, my parents never told me. Mentioning his name was enough to scare me right back into place. I didn't even want to know what he looked like, so I made it up.

"Well," I said, "he's tall, really tall, and he wears a gas mask with big round eyes, like a bug, that covers his entire face. He dresses in a shiny black uniform, blacker than you can imagine, and a long black cape hangs on his back."

"Like a superhero?" my son asks.

"No, like a supervillain. Hidden underneath the mask and armor, the bogeyman is covered in scars and burns. They say he can walk right through fire and feel no pain. Yet his body can still be burned."

"Where did he come from?"

"Nobody knows. All anyone knows is he shows himself to little children who don't listen to their mommies and daddies."

"Did he ever take you?" my son asked.

"Almost," I said. "I was a very naughty boy. One night when I was sleeping, the bogeyman showed up and tried to take me away, but grandma and grandpa rushed into my room and begged him not to."

"What did he do?"

"He told them, 'I have come for your child for he has disobeyed you; he will be mine.' They cried and begged him not to take me away from them. So he looked at my parents and said 'He has one more chance left, and if he fails once more, you will never see him again.' I awoke up the next morning, and ever since, I've never disobeyed my parents."

"I don't want the bogeyman to take me, daddy." He pouted.

I smiled. "Don't worry, he won't take you as long as you're a good boy and you do what you're told."

In fairness, I shouldn't joke. This isn't some kind of scary bedtime story; it's real. The image of the bogeyman I had come up with was eerily accurate. I thought I had made up his description, but I realized I had seen him before—except, during that time, I knew him by another name.

I was ten, maybe twelve. The Vietnam war had just ended and my father had come home. When I say that my father had told me some of the most horrific stories I've ever heard, you have to believe me.

A week before he left Vietnam, he had seen the Maskman on the battlefield. I remember my father describing it, the fear in his eyes, and the wavering of his voice, I had never seen him this agitated, this afraid. The Maskman—he was just standing in the fires, watching. My father was with the company of four other soldiers; yet, no one else had seen the man. And if you had gazed into my father's eyes, you'd know he wasn't lying.

My father had glanced down at the muddy ground, and when he looked back up, everything was gone—the Maskman, the other soldiers, the enemy. Before he knew it he awoke in a hospital bed, with no trace of the other four soldiers. Were they even real? They damn sure existed.

You might be asking yourself, why was the Maskman on a battlefield, isn't he merely a character in a children's story?

The Maskman doesn't care about the children, who tell themselves stories to make themselves feel better. Children *romanticize* things. He has been around for longer than you've known.

The night after my father told me his story, I was in bed, right on the edge of sleep. In the darkest corner of my room, I could see his silhouette—the Maskman, accompanied by four other men in uniform.

The bogeyman grows with the child into the Maskman. The true form of the Maskman is that of a terrible omen. It is a sign, a warning. It spares no one, no child, no woman, no man. It is the lull before the storm, the parasite of the mind. This Maskman, a ghastly appearance molded to your fears.

My son needed to be aware of the Bogeyman's taunts and now has to face the terrors of the Maskman. Many may experience the horrors of the Maskman— to overcome, you'll have to look beyond it to escape it before it overpowers you.

35

GLASS CASE

by Jacqueline Nguyen

Pain and emotions I've held within
Felt as if my fragile heart would shatter
My love, my entire being,
Ached to be with him
I wanted to be his haven.

He seemed empty inside,
Alone, delicate, vulnerable,
I couldn't bear to see him like this,
Fragile moments of him,
His vulnerability,
This precious work of art,
I thought,
Must be protected.

WHEN THE SUN COMES DOWN

by Valerie Nguyen

When the sun comes down
I find myself crawling to the rooftop
With a notebook in one hand
And a blanket in the other.

When the sun comes down
The tears start to fall
The loneliness engulfs me
And I sit in silence
with the thoughts that hurt me.

When the sun comes down
I begin to wonder
When will it all end
For the pain is too great.

When the sun comes down
I awake from my dreams
Always remembering
The peace it brings me.

The pain always stays
The tears always fall
The love never leaves.

But that's only
When the sun comes down.

BREATHE

by Michelle Lam

It was unnoticeable at first.
When the little damp spots had covered the floor
And I thought a little was alright
But more gathered and pooled
Lapping at my legs
Begging me to change
A blind eye to it until discomfort
Problems start to cover my legs
Torso
Shoulders
Neck
A sharp chill struck my spine
And I panicked
As fear enveloped me
Pressuring me underneath
Now all too much
And I want to forget
Think of nothing
My body submerged in icy water
Filling my lungs
Numb with a throbbing, aching pain
But through the blurry, stinging ocean
There were clouds and warm sunlight
That I never noticed before
Blanketing my body with slight ease
My stiff, frozen fingers could reach it
I could almost touch it
And I finally felt
I wanted to breathe

MARIGOLD

by Jacqueline Truong

"Come and live with me"
You speak
in a whisper,
Hushed, but delicate
Your words are silken,
enlaced with sugar,
but their meanings
are ever transient.

"I'll stay if you love me"
I speak,
or rather, plead
as you, my dearest, are
the beautiful flower,
and I, your love,
am a weeping honeybee
numbed with sorrow.

"Stay and die with me"
You speak,
beckoning me,
with flightless wings
The wind billows,
a pathetic attempt to cushion
my fall to the world below
enlivening the marigold.

My Friends Are Food

by Diane Bui

Pumpkin Pie

He's the popular one,
In every room, brings a smile, a laugh,
So simple, so delightful, so warm.
Connects people together in joy and memory,
Loving and sweet.

Blueberry Tea

She's warm and loving.
Her voice so soothing, so calming, so pure,
It alleviates me of my harshest tensions.
Her smile alone brings a soft pleasure,
The sweetness She carries marks the birth of my smile

Lemonade

He's the simplest and most independent
Alone He is sour, yet by holding hands He is sweet,
A sugary smile melts the heart.
His beautiful mind, chill and collected,
I search for him when I need to cool.

AS YOU WALKED BY

by Aysha Pena

As you walked by
With your head held high

I was blinded by your light

I kept walking by
Keeping my head low

Afraid to meet your eyes

I know you will never be mine
And that's fine
I'll keep my feelings inside

But just know that one day
If I meet your eyes
I'll ask you stay

And one day
You'll grab me by the waist
And say "Be my only light"

But right now I'll just wait
When you come my way
And I'll just keep it within

SPECIAL DELIVERY

By Valerie Nguyen

CHARACTERS

SPORTSCASTER MIA: adult female
DELIVERY MAN BLAKE: adult male, clumsy, nervous, forgetful
MOTORCYCLIST: adult male
OFFICER ISAAC: adult male
AIRPORT GIRL: adolescent female, FLUFFY's owner
FLUFFY: Maltese dog
PRESIDENT: adult male

FADE IN:

INT. AIRPORT TERMINAL-MORNING

MIA and **BLAKE** are standing by the baggage claim, the camera pointed at them. People walk and do their own business in the background.

> MIA
>
> Good morning, America. I'm glad you are tuning in with us today for a special delivery to the president from the princess of Thailand, Maha. We have Blake who will be delivering this very important package. Say, Blake, what exactly is inside? Everyone's dying to know.

> BLAKE
>
> Well, supposedly there is a golden elephant statue.

> MIA
>
> Real gold? Wow, that is a huge responsibility. How do you feel about that?

Blake is visibly sweaty.

                    BLAKE
        I'm really nervous. I don't think I'd be able to pay off the debt if
        anything were to happen to it.

                    MIA
        I think we can tell by your sweat.

                    BLAKE
Oh, no!

Blake wipes sweat from his face and covers his armpits.

                                    SMASH CUT TO:

EXT. AIRPORT TERMINAL-MORNING
Mia is standing in front of the delivery truck with **OFFICER ISAAC**, the camera
pointed at them. Other officers and people are in the background, some walking
or standing.

                    MIA
        Moving on, we also have Officer Isaac and his partners following
        Blake for security.

        Officer Isaac, how are you feeling about your task? It's a short
        20-minute drive to the White House, correct?

                    OFFICER ISAAC
        Yes, that's right, and I'm confident that we can get this package
        to the White House in one piece. I've never had a difficult time
        with any job that I've been given.

                    MIA
        That's quite the confidence, Officer. Let's hope that luck of yours
        gets the package safely delivered.

                         43

OFFICER ISAAC

Of course, it will.

Enter Blake. He is carrying a box in which the gift to the president is in.

MIA (O.S.)

It looks like we're getting ready to get going. Wait, what's going on there?

Enter **FLUFFY**. Fluffy is biting and pulling on Blake's pant leg.

BLAKE

Get off me you evil dog. I'm carrying an expensive statue.

MIA (O.S.)

Oh no, it looks like Blake is struggling with that little white dog. Let's hope he doesn't drop the package.

BLAKE

Get this dog off of me, Officer Isaac!

MIA (O.S.)

Someone should really help the guy.

Enter **AIRPORT GIRL**. She is running toward Blake and Fluffy. Her face is blurred for privacy reasons.

AIRPORT GIRL

I'm so sorry! Fluffy get over here.

MIA (O.S.)

Can we get the audio on Blake rolling?

BLAKE

I could sue you for that! If I dropped this package, you would be the one paying   for it.

AIRPORT GIRL

Geez! I already said sorry. It's not like I wanted this to happen!

MIA (O.S.)

Things seem to be heated between Blake and that little girl. Her face is turning extremely red.

Airport girl clenches her fists.

MIA (O.S.)

Uh oh, this doesn't look good.

Airport girl punches the box.

BLAKE

Are you insane, kid? Do you know how much this thing costs?

AIRPORT GIRL

No, and I don't care! I hope you lose your job. (stomps foot)

MIA (O.S.)

That was harsh. Who knew the girl would have such a nasty side.

AIRPORT GIRL

Let's go, Fluffy. (Tugs Fluffy's leash)

MIA (O.S.)

It looks like she wants to leave... Wait, zoom in on the dog. Fluffy barks and urinates on Blake's leg.

BLAKE

Ew! What in the world? Your dog just peed on me.

AIRPORT GIRL

You deserved it.

MIA (O.S.)

That was interesting... The package has barely left the airport and Blake is not on Lady Luck's good side. This is definitely going to take longer than it should.

Blake puts the box in the delivery truck.

> MIA (O.S.)
> Finally, it looks like we're heading out now. Let's go follow the truck in our van.

CUT TO:

INT.-NEWS VAN-MORNING

Mia is sitting in the passenger seat and looking out the window. The camera is positioned to look outside another window in the van.

> MIA (O.S.)
> Washington's streets are sure beautiful but are so narrow. I wonder if that'll be a problem for such a truck like Blake's when turning.

Enter **MOTORCYCLIST**. He attempts to cut off Blake after turning.

> MIA (CONT'D, O.S.)
> Would you look at that? This is not looking good at all. There's a speeding motorcycle trying to cut off Blake.

Officer Isaac has motorcyclist pull over. Blake brakes in the current lane.

> MIA (CONT'D, O.S.)
> Did you hear that? There was a loud thud coming from the back of the truck from Blake's hard braking. I wonder if he'll ever be handed a task like this again after today's events.

> MIA (CONT'D, O.S.)
> Can we get audio from Officer Isaac's body cam?

> MOTORCYCLIST
> I didn't do anything wrong, Officer.

> OFFICER ISAAC
> You were going 60 miles per hour in a 40 miles per hour zone. You'll be receiving a ticket for that.

                    MIA (O.S.)
Cut to Blake, he's getting out the truck.

                    BLAKE
It's only a 20-minute drive for this dumb package. Why is the
world against me today? I've never had this much trouble with a
delivery before! It's like I'm cursed today. The statue is supposed
to be good luck.

                    MIA (O.S.)
Blake is fuming as he's checking on the package. The package
looks perfectly fine and Blake seems relieved. I wonder if he's
regretting taking this job.

                    BLAKE
I'm only five minutes away from the White House. What else
could go wrong?

Birds fly over and defecate on Blake.

                    MIA (O.S.)
Yikes, he spoke too soon. Some birds just dropped some feces on
his head.

Blake kicks the truck multiple times and yells at the birds.

                    MIA (O.S.)
I think after today Blake will need some mindfulness sessions.
He's kicking the poor truck like it's at fault. Motorcyclist leaves
with his ticket. Officer Isaac walks up to Blake and places a hand
on the delivery man's shoulder.

                    OFFICER ISAAC
Sorry to break it to you buddy, but I'm going to have to give you
a ticket.

                    BLAKE
What? A ticket?

OFFICER ISAAC

You're holding up traffic. (points to the side of the street) You're supposed to park by the curb if you're going to stop. Right now, you're parked in the middle of the right turn lane.

Cars are honking at Blake. One driver shown with a blurred face flips off Blake that too is also blurred.

BLAKE

I swear this job is the absolute worse.

SMASH CUT TO:

INT.-NEWS VAN-MORNING

Blake is stomping toward the news vans.

MIA

Why is Blake coming over here? He looks extremely angry. I'm locking the doors.

Blake knocks on the van window Mia is in front of.

BLAKE

Where's the damn camera?

MIA

(rolls down window)
Right here. Why? Is there a problem?

BLAKE

(shows the camera his ticket)
Do you see this ticket? You're the one paying. If not then the president will. I'm not taking responsibility for this ticket.

Blake stomps back to his van and starts for the White House. It can be seen from inside the news van.

MIA

It really just isn't his day, but on the bright side, we're only five minutes away from the White House. Let's hope the rest of the trip goes smoothly.

PAN over White House

MIA (CONT'D, O.S.)

Isn't it beautiful? I can't wait to see the statue when the president opens it. Ladies and gentlemen, you will be the first to see the president's gift.

CUT TO:

EXT.-WHITE HOUSE-MORNING

Enter **PRESIDENT**. He is waiting in the driveway. Mia is standing a distance apart from the president. The camera is pointed at her with the president in the background.

MIA

As you can see, the president's waiting here to retrieve his package.

Blake exits the truck and takes out the package. He carries it to the president and places it by his feet. He also pulls out the ticket from Officer Isaac. The camera is now pointed at them.

BLAKE

I don't know who is going to take care of this ticket, but it's definitely not me.

PRESIDENT

No worries, man. I'll take care of it. Thank you for delivering my chair in one piece. It's a unique antique from Princess Maha.

MIA (O.S.)

Yikes, Blake might have been overly stressed for no reason.

BLAKE

Chair? I thought it was a gold statue.

49

PRESIDENT

Gold statue? No, what are you talking about? Oh, my secretary actually believed that story? I was only joking. I'm happy to know you took great care of it, though. If I have another important package in the future, I'll be sure to hire you!

MIA (O.S.)

Blake looks so blank-faced, but I think the president is enjoying this.

BLAKE

Another package? Hire in the future? Oh no, no thank you! I quit!

Blake throws his hat on the ground and stomps on it. He gets back inside his truck and drives away.

MIA (O.S.)

I don't think he'll ever want to take this kind of job again.

Mia moves closer to the president and stands next to him. The president looks in the direction Blake took off in.

PRESIDENT

He isn't serious about quitting, is he? I feel a little bad now.

MIA

I think he'll be okay, Mr. President. He's just had a rough day.

MIA (CONT'D)
(looking into the camera)

Well, there you have it, folks. It was a wild journey to only find out that the alleged gold statue was only a joke made by the president, and that the package is actually a unique antique chair from the princess of Thailand. Let's hope Blake has better luck in the future and thank you, viewers, for tuning in with us today.

(PAN over the White House)

FADE OUT

LIVING IN THE PURPLE OCEAN

by Daniela Solano
(Dedicated to the left wing)

I spend so much time thinking of my boys.
a composition of cells, bone, and flesh,
yet their souls are beyond this lifetime.
their songs of struggle
of striving for better days,
of self-awareness,
the perfect recipe for loving another.
I stand, teary-eyed and anxious
with sweaty hands holding a flickering light,
standing in the purple ocean.

a day to let out the screams I've kept
from long school days,
where I can be with people like myself,
where I can listen to loving words
in limited English instead of,
through cheap headphones,
a day where I won't be questioned
about my music choices,
where I can really love myself,
where I can see the people
that saved my youth,

and a day where I swim in the purple ocean.

A VOICE

by Diane Bui

GREENERY HUNG FROM THE ceiling of the glass greenhouse, and lush emerald-green trees reclined on either side of the building. Glass vases of red and white flowers lined the walkway. Guests sat in black chairs on either side of the flower-lined aisle. The priest stood in the front, draped in his holiest garb, holding a black leather Bible.

Red and white rose petals graced the aisle with guests seated alongside. Three little girls flung velvety petals while they danced their way past. Melissa, a young woman in a lacy wedding gown, linked arms with her middle-aged mother, Vanessa, from the back of the room. The organ's soulful pitch sang the Wedding March; soft thumps of high heels and swishes of the bride's wedding gown kissed the aisle as the mother-daughter pair proceeded down the aisle.

Vanessa grinned and whispered, "It's a good thing your father isn't here on your special day, isn't it, sweetie?"

The bride kept her hazel gaze on the groom and the altar ahead. Gray clouds slowly loomed over the greenhouse, casting a shadow over the wedding.

Vanessa nudged her. "Melissa."

"Yeah….Yes, it is, Mom." Melissa's fingers fidgeted with the satin ribbon that bound her bouquet together. "I still wish he was here though."

Vanessa scoffed. "That old man has no right after what he did to us."

Melissa looked down at her bouquet of red and white peonies. Her mother had chosen that arrangement. A small frown spread across her lips. "I guess you're right, Mom."

Upon reaching the altar, Vanessa kissed her daughter's cheek and took her place in the second row of black chairs. Melissa handed her bouquet to her maid of honor. Her face flushed a rosy pink as the groom, Henry, held her hands in his. He gave her a faint smile.

The priest cleared his throat. "We are here today to celebrate the beautiful union of Mr. Henry Robinson and Ms. Melissa van Buren; two young people brought together in the holy sacrament of matrimony by the will of God. Are there any objections to this marriage?"

"I object," a strong and clear voice said. A middle-aged man rose from his seat. "I very much object."

A wave of shock buzzed through the guests. Vanessa rose from her seat, her face tomato-red and twisted by a deep scowl. "I told you to never come here, Stewart."

"Dad?" A wide smile leaped onto Melissa's face.

"Melissa, I need to talk to you," Stewart said.

"No, continue the wedding," Vanessa said. Melissa's parents continued their squabble.

Sighing, the priest shut his Bible closed and rubbed his forehead. "I think we could all take a break for Melissa's father to explain himself."

Stewart's shoulders relaxed. "Melissa, come with me. We have much to talk about."

"She will not come with you," Vanessa said.

"No. I want to listen to what Dad wants to say," Melissa said, her voice quivering. "Please. I haven't seen him in forever."

"Ten minutes." Vanessa threw glares as sharp as knives at Stewart then stormed away.

"Melissa?"

The bride turned to her groom, Henry. "I'm sorry. I have to talk to my dad. I won't be long, okay?"

"Will you be alright?" Henry glanced around the room. The guests were whispering amongst themselves, and from the corner of the room Melissa's mother scowled at her.

"I will."

"Are you sure?"

"Yes, I'll be fine."

"Call me if you need anything, okay?" He slid a hand into his pants pocket. "I'll just be around and looking at the trees or talking with some of the guests."

"All right," she said, ruffling his hair.

Father and daughter strolled through the greenhouse; morning glories brushed rosy Melissa's face as they walked.

"Why are you here, Dad?" She twiddled with the silk flowers sewn on her skirt. "I thought you didn't care about me."

"That's what I wanted to discuss." Stewart slid his hand into his jacket pocket and took a deep breath. "When your mother and I divorced, it was under the pretense that I had an affair with another woman. However, that story was false. Your mother fabricated that lie to divorce me."

53

"What?" Melissa's voice cracked. "But why?"

"Did you notice that your mother introduced you to Henry not too long after?"

"Well, yes," she said, "but he's such a good guy, Dad."

"He seems wonderful, but that's because your mother and his mother made an agreement between you two while you were only infants."

"What?" She stopped fiddling with the flowers. "So this was all a setup?"

"I'm afraid so."

"I don't understand." Melissa wiped a tear from her eye. "Henry? This? And you?" She shook her head. "Then why did you and Mom divorce?"

"I strongly opposed the decision. It wasn't right to decide on who you're marrying before you could even speak and think for yourself."

"Is that why Mom didn't let me see you?" Melissa asked, her voice strained.

"Yes."

"But why all this trouble?"

Stewart sighed. "Money."

"Money? There's no way." She fidgeted with the silk flowers again. "Mom wouldn't do that, would she? She always took care of me."

"Have you ever realized that not everyone can afford to go on nice vacations to Hawaii or such every summer? That on each and every trip, Henry and his family came along and it was never the two of you, you and your mother, alone?"

"Mom said that she had Henry and his family come along so we'd be closer as a bigger family."

"But she wouldn't want to be closer to her own daughter?"

"I don't know." Melissa stopped fiddling with the flowers and took a deep breath. She turned and approached the altar. "Henry?"

"Yes?" The groom turned to Melissa.

"Could you come here, please?"

Henry excused himself from his friends and family. Upon reaching Melissa and her father, he held out his hand.

"It's very nice to meet you, sir."

"Nice to meet you, too, kid." Stewart took Henry's hand and shook it.

"Did you need something, dear?" Henry said to Melissa.

She turned to her father. "Do you mind?"

"Of course not." Stewart left them alone and walked toward a planter filled with pink carnations.

Melissa sat on a bench and Henry sat next to her. She took another deep breath and folded her hands. Her eyes met his. "I know you don't really love me."

"What? What do you mean? Of course, I love you."

"My father told me everything."

Henry shifted in his folded his hands. "Oh."

"The money. The lies. The whole setup so my mother could have whatever she desired."

He looked away. "I only wanted to make my parents happy."

"I know now. It isn't your fault, but I'm hurt." She felt warm tears pooling in her eyes. "I thought I could trust my mother. I thought I could trust you, but I don't know anymore."

The tears rolled down her rosy cheeks, dripping onto the floor and on her gown.

"I'm sorry… I didn't think it'd hurt you this much." He rubbed her back then pulled his hand away. Melissa's father walked over to them and laid a hand on each of their shoulders.

Heels clicked on the ground as Vanessa stomped up to them, her arms crossed. "Time's up."

"Can't you see she's not ready?" Stewart said. "She needs time."

"No. Everyone else is waiting," Vanessa said in her shrill voice. "The wedding must go on now."

"Vanessa." Stewart stood firm. "She knows the truth. Let her make her own decisions."

"You leave right this instant." Vanessa slapped him.

"I'm not leaving my daughter behind," Stewart said, wincing from the pain. "I'm not letting her mother's greed for money ruin her life forever."

The wedding guests gasped and looked at each other, then back at Stewart.

"That's right everyone." Stewart raised his voice. "This entire thing is all a fake. A setup. A ploy for money."

"How shameful," Henry's uncle said.

"And I thought weddings were about love," Melissa's younger cousin said.

Disgruntled family and friends murmured to themselves. One aunt threw down her purse. Younger family members pulled out their phones. The priest, still by the altar, looked away and shuffled his feet.

"Why you, silly children." Vanessa kicked Henry until he stood up. "Move, boy."

She grabbed Melissa's wrists, wrenching the sobbing girl upward and pulled her toward the altar. "Come on, Melissa, do it for me, the one who took care of you all your life."

"Mom, no!" Her wrists stung from her mother's nails digging into her skin. "Let me go. Stop forcing *your* will on me. I don't want this."

"Yes. You. Do. You will be married now."

"Let her go." Stewart grabbed his ex-wife's hands and tugged them, freeing Melissa from her grasp. The woman whipped around and kicked her ex-husband's shins with her pointed heels.

"Enough is enough," he said. "She knows now. You can't stop it any longer."

"Yes. I. Can." Vanessa twisted and squirmed, failing to escape her ex's firm grip. Security guards rushed in and held Melissa's mother by the arms.

"Let go of me, you hooligans." She continued kicking and yelling obscenities as the guards dragged her from the venue. The clouds cloaking the greenhouse dispersed, allowing sunlight to shine on Melissa, Henry, and Stewart.

"Are you all right, Melissa?" Henry held her hands.

"A little shaken, but I'm all right."

"Again, I'm sorry," he said. "If you want to cancel this, we can. I don't want this to be forced. If you want, we could start again genuinely, or move on and find a different passion."

"I'd like that." She ruffled his hair. "A fresh start without strings attached. Thank you, Henry."

"It's settled then." A gentle smile bloomed on his lips.

Melissa turned to her father, teary-eyed and smiling, and embraced him. "Thank you, Dad, for coming here and telling me. For giving me a voice."

PUZZLE

by Jennifer Ho

He told me
I was confusing
That I didn't make any sense.
What was I to him?
A crossword puzzle?
I scribbled my frustration onto my palm—
But the ink ran out before my tears did.

LEARNING LANGUAGES

by Christine Vu

How do you pronounce this preposition?
Not asking for the definition.
One word translates to five
You'll get it if you strive
Alphabet is more than recognition.

YELLOW

by Bethanie Luu

Hanahaki /hônahəkē/ - (noun) an illness born from unrequited and/or unattainable love in which flowers grow within the lungs of the victim, causing for his or her airways to become clogged with petals; the only cure is to remove them surgically, resulting in a loss of feelings or memories for the love interest

YELLOW. IT WAS SUCH a beautiful color, such a happy color.

And as the little daffodil petals fell into his cupped hands, Yuuto only then realized that such happiness had a price. His throat felt raw from all the coughing and retching, and his chest ached with pain and pressure as if something were growing from within. When the last of his tears leaked from his eyes, Yuuto slouched to the floor hugging the flower petals to his chest.

Hadrien.

"Hey, Yuuto? Could I talk with you for a second?" Hadrien gestured to a chair at their dining table and propped his chin upon his hand, his brown hair hanging to the side. "You know Yumei, right?"

"Of course. She's my childhood friend." Yuuto pulled back a chair and sat, rubbing the sleep out of his eyes. He looked up as Hadrien slid his phone into Yuuto's hands, an image of a beautiful Yumei smiling displayed upon the small screen. "And?"

"Do you think I'll have a chance with her?"

Yuuto looked up to see Hadrien twiddling with his thumbs, a bright red blush apparent upon his cheeks. Right then and there, Yuuto felt his heart drop to his stomach. "I have to use the bathroom."

Yuuto stood from the table and stumbled into their bathroom. He barely pushed open the toilet lid after slamming and locking the door behind him when velvety yellow petals began to spill from his lips and his chest lighting on fire.

Why? Why did Hadrien have to be interested in his friend Yumei, not him?

And when the last petal fluttered from Yuuto's mouth, he felt light headed, barely feeling the burning of his throat and chest. He only saw the blood that laced the daffodil petals.

"Yuuto?" There was a knocking at the door. "Are you alright in there?"

Panic arose within his throat as Hadrien knocked again.

"Yuuto?"

Yuuto rose to his feet, desperately holding to the marble countertop to keep him steady. "I'm fine." He flushed the toilet. "Just having stomach issues is all."

I should be fine.

Memories of Hadrien smiling and the melodious sound of his laughter filled Yuuto's sleep deprived mind. The mere thought of Hadrien was simply enough to keep him awake.

Hadrien was the sun. He was the sun that caused the flowers within his lungs to bloom. Flowers of love. Unrequited love, that is.

Yuuto fell asleep with the taste of yellow upon his tongue.

Yuuto looked up as he heard the sound of locks clicking and the front door to his shared apartment push open. He was about to lower his gaze back to his phone when his eyes caught sight of long locks of inky black hair. His eyes widened.

"Oh, hey Yuuto." Hadrien entered with a young woman.

Yuuto eyed Hadrien's arm around the woman's waist. "Yumei?"

"Oh, right," said Hadrien, grinning sheepishly. "Turns out she kind of likes me, too."

Yumei slapped Hadrien's shoulder playfully, laughing at the little remark.

Yuuto sat frozen on the couch, feeling his throat clog with a familiar feeling. He only managed to press his lips together and nod before croaking a pained, "I need to lie down."

As he collapsed to the floor within the safety of his room, he readily held out his cupped hands. But this time, when Yuuto tried to cough up the brilliant yellow flowers, he nearly didn't recognize what they were. The petals were clumped together, coated and dripping with a warm crimson liquid. For hours he sat crumpled like that, the flowers constantly flowing out of his mouth like a bloodied yellow waterfall. Tears escaped his eyes as Yuuto tried to quiet himself, hearing the teasing and giggling sounding from outside his door.

Hadrien, what are you doing to me?

Sunlight gleamed off Hadrien's chestnut brown hair, which bounced with each step he took, and his lightly tanned skin glowed in the afternoon sun. Yuuto was mesmerized.

They were alone together this time, no significant others or childhood friends to interrupt their quality time. But even so, Yuuto still felt his heart ache as he tried to suppress the garden growing within him. He couldn't let Hadrien find out.

"Yuuto, what do you want to eat?" Hadrien said.

This jolted Yuuto out of his thoughts. "I don't know. You can choose."

Hadrien nodded and again beamed his bright smile at him.

The two eventually found themselves seated in a cramped booth in a secluded café. Yuuto took in the aroma of the roasted coffee beans in the air and the warm feeling of the yellow sunlight flowing in from the windows. They were the only ones there, save for a couple engaged in an intimate conversation and a few employees cleaning up. He felt at peace.

Yuuto rested his chin atop his palm, drinking in the way Hadrien's eyes twinkled as he talked excitedly. Yuuto ignored the way his heart ached every time Hadrien would bring up Yumei's name. And of course, Yuuto couldn't say anything, scared that Hadrien would discover the petals that leaked from his lips as they did every night when he would allow himself to cry.

He couldn't hurt Hadrien like that. He simply couldn't. He wanted to see Hadrien smile, even though Yuuto's flowers would eventually suffocate him.

Yuuto wanted to die knowing that the one he loved so much would still be happy, forever wearing a smile upon his beautiful face.

And he remembered when they were children, how they would spend hours upon end, playfully walking hand in hand along the hot pavement of sweltering summer days, how they would stand on the old bridge, pretending to be drunk adults as they took swigs from a single bottle of cheap soda and laugh as they chased each other down the sunny streets. All those memories were tinted with a soft yellow. Happiness.

"Yuuto?" A hand touched his. "Yuuto, are you all right?"

Yuuto's eyes snapped upward to meet Hadrien's, whose face was filled with worry and concern. Yuuto didn't notice the tears slowly making their way down his tinted cheeks until they made a soft *pat* on his denim jeans.

"I . . ." Yuuto's breath hitched within his throat as it began to clog with petals. He only managed to wheeze, "Bathroom."

He stood and ran to the restroom, not once looking back to see if Hadrien was watching him.

There was a ringing in Yuuto's ear as he sat in the silence of his bedroom. In fact, the whole apartment was silent and monochrome.

He was alone.

He felt empty without Hadrien with him, missing the feeling of security and warmth he had with him. He only had the daffodils growing within his chest to keep him company.

Yuuto walked into to Hadrien's bedroom, finding him searching desperately for something in a drawer. As his hand brushed across a soft cotton material, he tugged his arms out with his fingers gripped around the large yellow sweater. Tears began to form at the corners of his eyes as he pressed the fabric to his face, taking in the scent of the one he loved so much.

And as Yuuto stood, he felt lightheaded as his throat slowly clogged with flowers, blocking his airways. Yuuto desperately stumbled into the living room, still drunk off Hadrien's scent.

He didn't make it to the bathroom in time. He tried to cry out Hadrien's name, but it was muffled by all the yellow daffodils spilling from his cracked lips. The pain in his chest was even greater than before, combined with the aching in his heart. Tears and blood dribbled from his chin, dripping down to stain the yellow sweater still clutched in his grasp. He heaved, his breathing becoming more and more labored as his airways became blocked

And there was only one thing one his mind before he blacked out.

Hadrien.

THE HOUSE WAS EERILY quiet when Hadrien pushed open the door, causing it to creak on its frame. Something was off, and he could feel it.

By now, Yuuto would have at least greeted him, unless he was asleep. He decided that the other was probably sleeping.

But even as he walked to his bedroom, Hadrien couldn't shake the feeling that something wasn't right. He didn't know why.

Until Hadrien saw Yuuto, collapsed on the floor, his body halfway between his door frame and the hall. But that wasn't what made his stomach drop. It was the blood flowing from his mouth, dribbling onto the clumped yellow flower petals by his lips, and his chest was barely rising, hand still gripping onto what the male recognized as his favorite yellow sweater.

"911, what's your emergency?"

"My...my friend." Hadrien felt hot tears making their way down his paled cheeks. He gulped.

"Yes?"

"Flowers."

Yuuto, how long have you been hiding this?

"I'm sorry, sir. We can't get a hold of his parents." The nurse placed and hand on her chest to take a breath. "We'll do our best."

"But will he—"

"We'll do our best to save him." She frantically seated him down into a waiting chair, placing her hands on his shoulders. "But we need to remove those flowers immediately."

"I . . ." Hadrien knew that this was the only way he could save Yuuto, so why was he so hesitant?

He should have known. He should have known all the clues were laid out before him, but he was too busy to notice, too busy to notice that the one he cared for most was dying before his very eyes. Instead, he chased after Yumei, thinking that she'd be a replacement for Yuuto.

But he was wrong. Nothing could ever replace Yuuto's breathy laugh or bright smile. Nothing could ever replace the way his eyes lit up when he was excited or the way his ears would flush when flustered. Nothing could ever replace Yuuto. Hadrien realized that he loved him.

"Of course. Do what you need to do." Hadrien watched the nurse scrambled away, followed by the sounds of footsteps squeaking against the hospital floors and wheels rolling down the hall. He looked to his right, catching a glimpse of a familiar tuft of raven hair before he buried his head in his hands.

Live, Yuuto.

"We're losing him."

The surgeon's eyes flicked up at the monitor. He looked back down at the young man lying before him on the operating table. His eyes were grim as they scanned over the body. He took a step back.

The nurses around him met his eyes. They knew.

Because it was too late. Only a prolonged beep sounded throughout the room.

Goodbye.

HADRIEN AWOKE TO THE feeling of someone shaking his shoulder. His back was sore from sleeping on the hospital chair, and he'd forgotten where he was for a second. But that was when he recognized the woman standing above him. She still had her mask tucked under her chin.

Hadrien's eyes brightened with hope. "How is he?"

The nurse didn't respond.

"He's alive isn't he?" Hadrien's smile dimmed. "No, he has to be alive." He stepped closer, his breathing becoming faster. "You said you would save him."

She pressed her lips together, looking to the side to avoid eye contact.

"You said you would save him!" Hadrien now stood over her, fingers curling and uncurling as he tried to ignore the wetness pricking at the corners of his eyes. "Do you even know how much he meant to me?" By now he was starting to quiver, arms shaking. "You promised. You promised!"

"I'm sorry, sir," the nurse said, backing away from him. "We tried everything."

Hadrien, dropped to his knees and as he buried his face into his hands, his body convulsing violently. Waves of grief crashed over him, tears streaming down his cheeks as he took in shuddered breaths.

"I loved him."

The sheets were white, like Yuuto's skin. Even in death, he was still beautiful. But his skin lacked its lively blush that was always ever so present, and his hair looked matted and faded. Gone was the boy Hadrien loved so much.

But as he held Yuuto's cold hand in his own warm ones, he could help but allow his gaze to wander to the right. There on the table sat two magnificent daffodils, their yellow petals only just starting to brown.

Wilting.

How could something as beautiful as these flowers kill?

Only the sound of Hadrien's sniffles and hiccups along with the low hum of air conditioning could be heard in the room.

He turned his attention back to Yuuto. Never in his life had he thought that he'd be letting him go. He felt like crying again, but he knew he had no more tears left in the hollowness of his heart.

Hadrien could only think of the blurry memories they shared together, so full of happiness and warmth, of how they would spend hours on end with each other and how their fingers would brush against one another during their late night strolls under the face of the moon and its stars. How had he not known? He realized that he loved Yuuto too late.

And when he closed his eyes, he felt the velvety taste of yellow upon his tongue.

TALK TO ME

by Krista Phanpraphou

It's been a while,
and we need to talk
You and I,
we're off to a great start
After a while you pushed me away
Saying you're busy studying and I said, okay

Honestly, I was hurt
but will always be by your side
I'll stay during these tough times
We share tears of sadness with a pinch of joy
and sleep with each other,
phones next to our faces,
Looking at the screen to see your frown
turn into a cute smile

But at times, I wish we never met
I wish you would disappear,
And be erased from my head
However, we know that can't happen
Because, in the end,
We need to talk,
For you are more than a friend.

WHAT A DAY TO BE ALIVE

by Tiffany Le

What a day to be alive
Under the starlight so bright
People reach for them with all their might

Firecrackers pop in loud glory
People dance together to the beat of the drums
With joyous faces in colorful clothing so fun

Children run through the temple
With their masks and toys
Playing tag with those around them, all enjoy

What a day to be alive
A day where spirits come out to play
They mingle with guests who are unfazed

What a day to be alive
Hear the lions roar
Driving out those evil spirits
To allow for a more prosperous year

What a day to be alive
May luck and happiness
Be in your favor,
Another year well spent.

CAN YOU BELIEVE IT?

by Jessica Lai

Without warning, he's gone.
Two individuals, once one,
Now nothing more than
strangers.
The result of false love.

When one stops trying
When one is, over
Over with everything.
You can't believe he's gone.
Days pass and you think that you're over him,
but you're not.

Look around,
His shadow is still there.
You can still see him standing:
a gleaming smile filled with past joys
His laughter still resonates in your mind.
But as you blink twice, there's nothing.

It's difficult to deal with the hole he's created
Not just a hole in your heart,
But a hole rooted deep within your soul.

When you pass by him
Every damn day
act as if everything's fine,
in reality your heart aches more and more
Until the pain is suppressed with tender warmth.

I can't believe that he is gone.

THE PRINCESS, SNOW WHITE

by Kathy Pham

Ebony hair, fair skin,
Dark eyes, ruby lips
A young girl who would be cursed
To devour the poison
From the apple so velvet
It was thought of, unspoken

She stares so longingly
Upon the black vintage fence
For one day thereafter her prince
Would rescue her, hence
Though years went by
He did not come
So she stood alone

She heard news from her mother
Her mother, so vain
The prince is near death
The mirror portrayed

"God, this prince is useless"
The princess thought in disbelief
"From a faraway kingdom
He ventured to find me
Roaming through the forest
His mind blank and awry
He managed to get lost
He starved and he hungered
He found some strange mushrooms
Which he somehow
Ate and ailed poorly."

Why was the prince poisoned?
Why was the princess stuck
In a pool of her own anger
She ran, her dress in a knot

Escaping the castle of the Queen
Impatient with her time
The young savage princess
Sought for medicine
A measure to save the prince
From his own idiocy
His own crime

"If I don't do it, who else dares"
The princess rolled her eyes
Her heart a bright flare

She sought out the dwarves
Seven in total
Barged into their house
And screamed
"I'm a noble!"

Showering them with her money
Pretty immodestly to say the least
Bribing the dwarves to help her
This princess is too greedy

She obtained the medicine
And ventured to his kingdom
Her patience
A sharp contrast

Stomping into his room
She shoved it into his mouth
"I'm saving your life
Don't be uncouth!"

He healed, thanking her over
Again and again
"What can I do for you
My brave, my fair lady?"
For that was the only thing
He could truly commend

She wanted nothing
But his gratitude, it's true
"Also please add ten buckets
Of gold revenue"

Now she's rich
She's living her life
For this girl was none other
Than sweet, innocent
Snow White

@DNLASLNOHSK

by Daniela Solano

The day was June 24 in 2001,
The time when my parents felt as if they finally won.
A little gummy face with big eyes
Soon became weary with the deception
Of waking up for school before the sunrise.
She is taller than the average height, yet she's
Too scared to put up a fight.
She's a pretty big scaredy-cat, she'll admit.
There are many things she's bad at, she knows it.
Her arms may always look crossed, and her face may look ice cold.
But just so you know, one of her biggest fears is being left alone.

She spent thirty-one thousand hours listening to her favorite artists
        this year
Her parents found out and made a face that gave her fear.
She likes taking walks around the street, even though in the end her
        legs feel beat.
She continues to live this way, just to feel the wind hit her face and
        make her hair sway.
She always keeps a little notebook and a pencil,
And enjoys the time at three a.m. sitting in the dark, when the earth
        is quiet and gentle.

She and her friends are as free as the stars in a constellation,
Waiting for the right bus to the future, in the wrong station.
We stand, short and tall, for there are times when we fall.
They helped her relieve hopelessness; a big barrier
They taught her she doesn't have to be alone because
The more the merrier.
Sometimes after school, they walk in a trio, to get snacks and
        what-not.

She's out so much that she and her parents fought.
Yet, at the end of the day, she tends to think about the events.
Homework, jokes, gossip.
She lays on her warm comforter and dreams about the time she
        spent.

Mom, dad. Little and big sister.
Childhood memories filled with playing, candy, and fake food, now
        seems like a twister.
Countless play-dates with herself, she was taught and is still learning
        to love oneself.
Playing different people during the day, princess, superhero, mom,
        and self.
Nothing felt better than sleeping with her plushies and a night light,
With the moon shining gray at the end of the day.

Where to begin, the future of her end lies in her own hands.
Does she want to sit and study in one place or travel the lands?
She's tired, but not from sleep deprivation.
She tries to get some sleep, but her mind is in elevation.
So don't be alarmed, she'll find her place.
She always has a hopeful look upon her face.

BABY OF MINE

by Sophia Trejo
(Dedicated to my mom)

"Don't you cry. Now, dry your eyes," you whisper to me,
Let me stay in your arms just for a few minutes more
And sleep in till noon.
I'm too selfish to share you
Too afraid to let you go.
I'll stay close to your heart so we never part
Heads thrown back and cramps in our backs,
The laughter never ends.
What a dangerous duo we are.
You are my rock, and I'm here to let you know that I'm yours too
From my head to my toes
I'm not much and everyone knows.
You're everything to me and
I'm sorry I don't say it enough.
You deserve more and I don't supply
But that's when you wipe my eyes
And say "Don't you cry
Baby of Mine."

MOTHER

by Michelle Hoang

A female wolf stands alone on a rock
With her soft, silver fur
and piercing green eyes.

Only year ago did she lose her babe
She howls on the same rock every night
Hopeful that one day her baby would return.

She stands out there, sacrificing her comfort and time
She fears that her baby has died
That her baby doesn't want to be with her
Even though she knows that
She has and will never give up
Because she loves her baby
Because she is a mother

NIGHTMARE

by Jacqueline Nguyen

I was scared.
Scared of losing myself,
Scared of losing my friends.
I didn't know what to do.
These fears, and more,
Swam through my head at night.
Haunting me in my nightmares,
Never letting me sleep.
One night, I entered a particular nightmare.
Walked through an amusement park,
Looking up at the Ferris Wheel just a few feet away.
Around me, people bustling with happiness and laughter.
Little kids held their mother's hands
"Mommy, mommy! I want to go there next!"
Running towards the next ride they wanted,
My gaze followed them,
Curious about what they were going to do next.
The scenery around the children turned from lively colors
To black.
What just happened?
I stood there, frozen.
Felt a tap from behind my shoulder.
Turning, only to face a smiling clown.
"Would you like a balloon?"
In one hand, he pushed a balloon towards me.
In another, a shining dagger.
Beads of sweat rolled down my face,
And all I could muster:
A scream.
I pushed the clown away from me,
Running, running.

Running away from the clown
Not once looking back.
However fast I ran, though,
The clown would always calmly walk towards me,
Still smiling and only a few feet away.
The clown had caught up to me
Shoving the balloon at me,
"Take it."
"NO!"
I screamed.
Waking myself up.
"It's only a nightmare… it's only a nightmare,"
I said to myself,
Not noticing the dark shadow
Standing beside my bed.

THE HUNT

by Andy Cu

A THICK MORNING FOG blanketed the foliage covered soil; the succulent scent of morning dew permeated the forest. The pale sun had just risen above the feeble horizon, painting the pine trees in a gentle, white light.

Upon one of the pines, a hunter sat, camouflaged by the plentiful ferns that engulfed him. The man's name was Walter; he was an adept specimen, more of a predator than a human. He had the heart of an ox and was muscled like a bear but with the agility and swiftness of a fox. Years upon years of hunting had toned his arms and left the skin of his hands rough whilst sharpening his mind. With his unbreakable will and unfaltering intellect, he felled all prey he set his eyes upon.

He wore simple garments made of cloth and hide, with the only exception being his long drab green cloak that covered almost the majority of his body and head. Lean leather boots adorned his feet and shins, scratched and worn throughout countless hunts.

His equipment was simple but effective, optimized for taking down prey, large or small. Tucked in his belt was a dagger with a razor sharp blade, used for everyday tasks like woodwork and food preparation. His hands clutched a finely crafted longbow, its wooden arms coated in a rich dark finish and bent rather violently into a subtle "U". This allowed the bowstring to be taut, allowing only a much trained arm to operate it.

Slung over the hunter's shoulder was a leather quiver stuffed with a dozen or so expertly made arrows. Each arrow was skillfully made; all were feathered with pristine quills. At the end of every arrow was a smithed arrowhead, stiff and slim, the ends as sharp as a sewing needle. These arrows, called bodkins, were specifically made to hunt prey with thick hide, or in Walter's case, light to medium armor.

He wasn't hunting a mere beast today; he was hunting the most cunning of all prey. Undoubtedly dangerous, they were crafty, ruthless, and had a knack of causing immense pain and suffering to those around them. He was hunting human this morning.

Walter had always despised humans, and he had every reason to. Humans including himself. The problem with humanity is that it always craves more, its very essence imbued with greed.

That was why he left his kingdom. His parents were wealthy merchants that lived leisurely in Lendric, the capital. As a young boy, he was entitled to a rich, noble adulthood. But he rejected wealth. Witnessing all the greed and injustice that occurred in the city, he fled in the night.

He brought nothing with him besides a small dagger and the clothes on his hide. He ran deep into the woods, and when he could run no more, he settled, and started to build his new home. He changed his last name. He wouldn't need it anymore. No one searched for him, because these woods were rumored to harbor unnatural beasts, making this area the perfect place for him to reside.

But as of late, these humans had begun to creep into the forest, as if they were searching for something. To protect his home, he fell them in their tracks leaving their corpses for the wolves. It may seem inhuman to do such a thing, but that was his goal, to distance himself from humanity as much as he could.

He desired to meld into the background, to melt into the peaceful continuation of nature. Some considered nature as chaos, as it bore no laws or regulations, but this state was the state that humans were intended to inhabit, so what was the reason not to relish it?

A sudden movement caught his eye—down a small beaten trail came two soldiers, both protected by fine chain mail, which covered every part of their bodies excluding their faces and boots. The one in front clutched a sheet of parchment, peering at it, most likely a map. The one that trailed behind stared into a compass. At both of their waists were long swords, sheathed in leather scabbards.

Walter inspected his quarry, memorizing their features, the way they moved, any information he could perceive with his eyes. He marked his prey, sealing their fates. They were sure to be dead within the hour.

His eyes tracked the two, rarely blinking, until they were mere meters away from the tree where he sat perched. Without making any sudden movements, he raised his bow with his left hand and drew an arrow with his right. Notching the arrow he pulled the bow up and aligned the tip with the front man's chest, all in one fluid motion.

As the soldier neared closer, Walter utilized his muscled shoulders to pull back the bowstring. At the flick of a finger, he could send the arrow into the man's torso. But he waited.

It would be much more efficient if he did, and efficiency was what he strived for. His prey was now below him. He drew a deep breath, trapping the air in his lungs. There was a tense, almost painful silence before he let the arrow loose.

The projectile soared downward at an angle, its feathers keeping its trajectory precise whilst making a faint whistle. The narrow bodkin point embedded itself into the man's chest, breaking clear through the chainmail and piercing through his flesh. A small stream of crimson liquid squirted from the puncture as the man dropped the map, his eyes widening. His entire body went stiff as he tried to let out a scream but couldn't, signaling that the bodkin had punctured a lung. The man fell onto his side, now a corpse.

Walter let out his long held breath, freeing up the space in his chest. The other was beginning to flee, screaming. He didn't even bother to check on his comrade or to draw his sword. All he saw was an arrow erupting from the trees and impaling his friend. It made complete sense that he ran.

But Walter could not allow him to live. The hunter leaped from the pine, landing onto the ground beneath with a subtle thud. Using his well-trained legs, he raced after his prey, each stride being deliberate and using the least amount of energy possible. While sprinting, he stuck his arm into the space between the arms of the bow and the bowstring, bringing it to his shoulder. Now wearing the bow like a parcel, he drew his dagger from its sheath and positioned the blade pointing downwards into a stabbing position.

Walter was gaining on his prey, his heavy chain mail lowering his stamina and slowing him down. Once Walter was a mere foot behind the soldier, he propelled himself towards the man's legs, arms out. Grabbing the soldier's legs in a bear hug, he brought his prey to the ground.

The two struggled for dominance on the ground, each using every muscle in their body to remain on top. But Walter's body was more optimized. Putting the soldier in an arm lock, he positioned himself on top, straddling him. Using both hands, aided by gravity, he pushed his dagger down towards the man's throat.

The soldier grunted in panic, planting his hands on Walter's pushing them away with all his might. The blade inched ever so closely to his throat, both men pouring their last bits of energy in this last struggle.

Then, still applying pressure onto the soldier, Walter changed his position so that he could use his weight to aid him. All the sudden he used all of his mass and pushed onto the blade. Finally, the soldier's arms gave way. The sharp blade buried itself into the soldier, crimson painted the soil below. He gasped for air and his eyes rose into the back of his head as he grunted his final pleas. He went limp.

Walter stood, examining his kill. Usually he would leave the corpses to be scavenged by the wildlife, but this time, he spotted a small round object tied to the man's waist. He crouched down and grasped it, using the edge of his bloodied dagger to free it from its tether. It was a ball about the size of his fist, made of some blackened glass. Protruding from the top was a small cylindrical cork, pushed into what seemed to be a nozzle.

As curiosity got the better of him, Walter pinched the cork, and with some effort, popped it off. All the kit contained was this fine dark powder, almost like soot. Bringing the nozzle to his nose, he smelled it, letting the aroma dance inside his nostrils. Its scent was harsh, punishing his curiosity as it permeated his clothing. It was gunpowder, a relatively new invention at the time that he'd left Lendric. It was truly a creation of man, unstable and volatile, with the capability of detaching limbs with just a pinch of its substance.

What were Lendric's people planning, sending out mere foot soldiers into the woods with such a precarious weapon? He thought of it logically, the only reason a kingdom would be issuing such a perilous contraption to its soldiers is if they were trying to kill an unnaturally powerful prey. Could it be himself? No, it couldn't, he was pronounced long dead by now.

Then he recalled the rumors of these woods, unnatural beasts made their homes here, or so they say. Was a well-developed Kingdom really on a wild goose chase in order to find and kill beasts that never existed?

No, Walter recalled the King of Lendric, father McDonnell. He was cunning and cruel, but intelligent nonetheless. He was a well-educated man; the only way he'd issue such an order is if there was an active threat within the area.

It then donned on him that an alarming amount of deer and fawn had been slaughtered by some predator as of late. It wasn't normal, but was feasible that a pack of wolves might've gotten lucky in the past few weeks. But the wounds that the stags had sustained did not follow the usual signs of a wolf pack attack. These wounds followed the routine of a single predator, and a large one at that. Each deer he found bore a couple long, deep gashes, made by an adept pair of claws. Maybe McDonnell was searching for this beast, trying to eliminate a threat before it became a larger threat.

If that was so, it would only be fair if Walter hunted it first. It affected him in no way, but he was willing to risk his life just to spite McDonnell. His prey this time was powerful, he could tell, as it could compete with the bears and packs of wolves native to this region. From what he could gather, his quarry was a large beast that utilized its claws on the hunt. It was not unlike a bear in that sense, but Walter could sense something was wrong, a certain balance in the humors told him so.

If this was true, bodkins would not do; his prey more likely than not had soft hide, so a wider point would serve him better. As he arrived home, he started to change out his gear. He put down his longbow and opted for an experimental weapon. It was a large, unwieldy great bow, taller than he was. This type of bow was unique, meant for felling mythical wyverns and dragons, but those were merely tall tales. It was so impractical that he doubted its ilk had meant to see any practical use at all, but rather as a meaningless decoration.

But this one, he had smithed himself, more of a product of boredom and curiosity than of actual necessity, it had been sitting on his wall for months. But today, it would see use. Some key features set this specimen apart from its decorative and useless brethren.

Inside the bow's polished oak arms, lay an iron rod, flexible enough to budge when moved, but stiff enough to provide extreme resistance. The bowstring was made of about a dozen miniscule iron threads, intertwined into a helix as to reinforce it. These factors combined made the draw weight of the bow ungodly, firing it would be like lifting a wagon with one arm. That was what Walter had in mind while smithing it.

Its arrows in question were also especially made for it. The arrows were longer, thicker. The quills feathering them were plucked from a great flachon, making them hard and stiff. The arrowhead was massive, about the size of his hand, and made of hard iron. It was smithed into a triangular shape, with its arms pulling far back, making it so that when it entered flesh, it would be nearly impossible to rip it out without tearing out a sizable chunk of flesh.

This bow and arrow combination created the strongest takedown bow in the kingdom. It was strong enough to bring bears and moose down with complete ease. If it were to hit a human, they would be thrown multiple feet backwards, killing them the moment the arrowhead decimated their organs. In short, it would do.

He lifted the bow from its rusted hinges and strapped it to his back; the weight of the weapon was so intense that he nearly stumbled when attempting to walk with it. He then grabbed three arrows, as that was all that fit into his quiver.

Now it was time to track his quarry, if this was a large beast, it would have had to leave a distinct trail. He put himself in the position of his prey, it was intelligent enough to avoid being killed or captured for weeks, so it would attempt to find a safer area to hunt. That would mean that it traveled higher up, most likely atop a hill. It also needed an abundant food supply and plenty of foliage to successfully hunt.

A high area that was wooded and fostered a decent amount of deer or other livestock. This was a perfect description for Carsus Peak. It was a little known hill, more of a shallow mountain that jutted from the lush forest beneath it. It was forested, harboring an almost alarming amount of fern and pine. It was also one of Walter's premier stag hunting areas.

It was a mere league or two away from his residence, so the trip wouldn't be a problem. The problem was his prey would be on high alert, sensing many people were trying to take its life. Instead of sprinting there, Walter decided to take the safe route and utilized a fox trot. A style of movement that allowed its user to tread on light feet throughout the foliage covered woods, whilst still allowing a decent speed.

It was nearly midday now, and the forest was now showered in a harsh, orange light. As he neared the peak, he began to hear a ruckus, the closer he came to the source of the noise, the more it sounded like a battle. Then he encountered the affair.

Walter dropped onto the ground; he lay motionless, engulfed in a thick brush as he examined the scene that played out before him. The first thing he noticed was a massive writhing mass of fur and fangs. It was more than twice the size of a bear but moved as quickly as an elk. Although covered in hide, its features were uncannily reptilian. It had a narrow head with rows upon rows of razor teeth, a small, almost glowing crimson eye protruded from both sides.

Its four legs were powerful, as even through the hide, you could see rippling muscles. It had hands similar to a primate, even having opposable thumbs, but jutting from them were gargantuan, razor sharp claws. Its body was similar to a lizard, and its tail thrashed. Its body was disproportionate, with its head being nearly as large as its body. The most disproportionate aspect about its body was its huge neck; it looked like a huge bulbous mass of muscle and sinew.

It was the most powerful specimen Walter had ever laid eyes upon. It was battling half a dozen soldiers, dressed the same as the ones Walter had previously dispatched. They wielded long spears, trying to keep the monstrosity as far from them as possible. They poked and prodded, puncturing the beast an infeasible amount of times, but the beast kept thrashing about, screeching and snarling as it did so.

At some point, the soldiers turned to their last resort, the fire bombs that they had been equipped with. One soldier drew one from his pouch and lobbed it at the beast.

When the bomb made contact with the beast, it shattered, plastering the powder all over the beast's thick fur. Then the second stage commenced, a small spark emitted from the cork of the bomb. When it touched a single granule of gunpowder, it erupted into a brilliant outburst of destruction. Fire spewed out in every direction, but the blast was concentrated on the beast's fur. The volatile liquid fire enveloped the monster's thick locks, causing it to dance erratically.

From the beast's gullet came a screech, a shrill scream that sounded almost humanlike. The screech sliced through the air, assaulting the ear drums of any organism that surrounded it, the ground shook and rumbled at the force of the outcry.

This was the prime time to strike, his quarry was weakened. With great care, Walter took the great bow of his shoulders, driving the end of one of its arms deep into the earth. Now that it was anchored, his strike would be more precise, for if he missed, he would be mauled. The sound of the bowstring snapping to its resting position would produce a sound that would resonate throughout the forest.

The creature still writhing in pain, Walter took an arrow from his quiver and notched it onto the stone stiff bowstring, grasping the bow with his left hand. Then, using every muscle in his shoulders and arms, he tugged the bowstring back. It barely moved an inch, and it felt like he was trying to bend an iron rod, but he kept pulling. Centimeter by centimeter, he inched the string back to his cheek and held it. It was excruciating, the steel threads were cutting through his thin leather gloves and into his flesh. His muscles felt as if they were going to snap, the tension was ripping at his ligaments and sinews.

The long oak arms, reinforced by flexible iron rods, were bent violently, and looked as they were about to snap at any moment. But nonetheless he set his sights on his prey. The gargantuan arrow tip now pointed at the beast's neck, if he could land a hit there, it would tear straight through its esophagus.

He then drew a long breath, strapping the air in his lungs. He went completely still. The beast was now rolling and writhing in the dirt, beginning to extinguish the flames. The men around it stood panicking, not knowing what to do. Walter calmed his mind, isolating the arrow and his prey, ignoring everything else around them. He let the bowstring go.

The arrow surged forward with so much power and force that the leaves around it were thrown into the air, the shock of the sudden release of energy traveled into his arms and all the way to his chest, shaking his very core. His knees buckled and he fell, bringing the bow down beside him. The projectile soared through the sky, its momentum battling gravity at every second, until it reached its target.

The broad tip sliced into the beast's hide like butter, burrowing deep into its muscled neck. Crimson liquid spewed in every direction, coating the soldiers in a vile, gruesome sludge. The beast attempted to screech again, but it couldn't, instead, muffled gurgling sounds came from deep within its maw.

Walter had hit the target; his quarry would soon fall from lack of oxygen.

But the beast didn't fall. As if from pure primal instinct and rage, it refused to perish, although it was being engulfed by the abyss of death, it fought against the chains of possibility. It stayed alive through pure, raw emotion.

The sight of such a horrendous beast succeeding in the fight to beat death itself was awe inspiring. Walter sat, wide-eyed at the phenomena that transpired before him. Its will to live, to survive was so prominent that it was almost visible. It was an animal that craved a free will of its own, but the cruelty of humanity was too much to bear. It slumped down, lifeless.

Walter gazed upon the scene before him; the ground was littered with gore and corpses, strung about haphazardly. Many lives were lost today, but at least the hunt was over.

The sun hung onto the horizon, painting the land in a gentle orange haze. The various fauna crept back into their homes, retiring for the night, and the woods grew silent. The more he pondered, the more Walter questioned his way of life.

There was no need to keep killing. The beasts of the forest would serve the same purpose with or without him.

The hunter walked between the trees as he dropped his weapons on the floor. He transformed. No longer a hunter, he would just be Walter.

Walter wandered into a new life, one without killing, maybe to become a potato farmer.

Where would he go next?

Even he didn't know.

OUR DARKNESS

by Iris Sanchez

It's a big world out there, filled with so many different faces.
In this never-ending sea of places I can't reach,
Take my hand and I'll lead you away from the darkness in your head.
I'll follow you, you'll follow me
Because you are the light that keeps me up at night
The sun that keeps me alive
You've become my world in such little time.
In this big world, I choose you.
This darkness of ours
wraps around our minds.

I start to suffocate, my light becomes dimmer
and I'm lost once again,
I'm not strong or brave enough.
Talk to me, let me hear your voice one last time,
make all these thoughts in my mind leave.
Let me hold you one last time before we leave.
Hold onto me and I promise never to let go,
I'll be your shield, your light, your smile
So turn around, I'll protect you from your darkness.

A TRAGEDY IN FOUR PARTS

by Kathy Pham

The Life,
A sweet dance
A love, blooming like flowers amongst two
A story, like a fairy tale
They stumble, they fall

An anxious grace in their steps
They laugh, they smile
Butterflies within their hearts
A couple bears their love
Like a ripened apple on a tree

How sweet the melody, how sweet the sound
They lay their lives
On the bare plains of their fields
Where they water their flowers

Where they waltz in a tale
Of Life
And their hearts

The Death,
A sorrowful parting
A sickness, incurable
A broken wing, torn

She twirls and falls, her heart
An empty hole
A gap, a glass vase
He cannot piece back together
They were ripped in two

A half of a whole

Their fields once golden
Yellow and blue
Now withered by the ocean
A dull gray hue

He sighs, was he a hero?
Was it all for naught?
He fought so many things,
Yet his wife remained with him not

They were a small couple
In the vast expanse of the world
He was a hero, and she, by his side
Stood proudly commending him

He dances a solo
Alone in his steps
For his heart no longer there
She had taken it with her

The Revival,
A trumpeting roar
A feared sorceress washes up ashore
She seems to be feeble
She seems to be weak

Yet in all of her ways
She is beautiful and sleek
A woman to behold

Yet he did not feel a beat
In his heart, he was hollow
Forever bleak
He fed her, he healed her

He offered his home
Yet to offer his crops
He would not

She felt her heart awaken
With an emotion so new
This witch has been dancing
All alone too

But with an unmatched duet
Came a broken misstep
He rejected her diamonds
And he embraced his old blooms

She, enraged to a fault
Cast out a spell
A spell of revival, but alas in reverse

There she stood, in all her glory
His once torn up half
Alive and yet mourning
She was not quite there, her eyes empty
She did not recognize him
But her tears felt quite salty

He watched in horror
As she took up a sword
For once he fought many
Now he must fight once more

The Sacrifice,
The finale
A bittersweet ending
One I fear telling
For it isn't compelling

He trembled in anguish
Unable to fight
How could he bear to—
Against his own wife?

His body was worn
His wings once shone bright
Were torn up and broken
Tiny shards in the night

She didn't understand
Why he smiled so warmly
Upon his deathbed
Yet it was a warning

Leave this place now
I'm sorry, I'm sorry
You should've stayed dead
And now you'll be lonely

His sweet caress
She'll never forget
For the man she once loved
Had left, wallowed in regret

A sorceress laughed
What a fitting end
A couple, how lovely
They dance and they mend
Now is the ending, now it is clear
A dance shall not last
Forever nor for years

The wife's heart was hollow
She could not comprehend
Her feelings were mingled

But she knew she had committed
A blunder she could not defend

She glanced at her sword
Gleaming a red and black
She aimed at the heart
She once found she lacked

This is the finale
You say so coyly
He was a hero, and I was his wife
And if that were so
I must end it
With my life

TRAITOR

by Nancy Huynh

The insertion of a chip into a newborn's brain has been law for centuries, a common practice that ensures safety and order amongst society. Some would rather kill themselves than live with violation of their body and opinions. The government simply calls this "natural selection." Perhaps those traitors were smarter than the rest.

"DID YOU HEAR ABOUT the robbery across the street?" Carrie asked, flipping through the channels on television.

"No, but the government will track their chip," Dan said.

Carrie set down her remote as a brightly lit and colorful advertisement interrupted her cooking show.

"Do you want to live free from government's watch, all for free? Sign up to partake in Operation Unchipped, in which participants live without the control of a chip in the brain for two days. World-known scientists have developed this phenomenon for centuries! Visit us at Mod Reef quickly because spaces are limited! This has been approved by—"

Static infiltrated the screen. Carrie stared at the television so intensely that she felt the light from the television heat up her face. She thought it was peculiar the "world-known scientists" were even allowed to oppose a system the government had strictly implemented for so long, let alone have an advertisement encouraging citizens to do the same. She turned to Dan to tell him her concerns, but the ringing in her head prevented her from doing so.

"Let's go," Carrie said. Her eyes grew wide, shocked at her own words. *No,* she wanted to say, but the pain in her head caused her to lie down on the couch silently.

"Okay," Dan said. He held his palm to his forehead and winced.

The two sat silently in the car. Occasionally, one would cry out in pain, and the other would glance over, only to cry out in pain as well. Other cars trailed by them, causing extreme traffic near the beach port, with a large and flashy sign reading, "Experience Mod Reef."

As people got out of their cars and the gates to the port began to close, a speaker called out, "Ladies and gentlemen, you have been chosen to be the lucky participants of Operation Unchipped, where you can finally be free!"

The crowd cheered. Gates to a large building opened, sending a swarm of people into the property.

Dan grabbed Carrie's hand and sent her a worried look. *I have a bad feeling about this.* Immediately, he kneeled over in pain.

"Dan…" *Run!* A shock swam through Carrie's brain, and a flash of light illuminated her head before she flew to the ground. Her pupils dilated and her neck jerked side to side, causing the words she tried to spew out to be nearly inaudible.

I have to get out of here. Dan winced, and he too, lit up from the shock of electricity. His eyes turned bloodshot red and bulged as he strained to speak. His lips twitched violently, and flames ignited on his head as he whispered his last words, "It's a trap."

A lone woman followed the crowd.

What's happening? Ana thought as she walked toward the burning pair. Their bodies were indistinguishable as the flames enveloped them. She wished to stop but her legs pulled her towards the gate.

As she followed the others closer to the entrance, she turned around and saw that men cladded in suits had rushed out to extinguish the flames.

The inside of the building was dark, save a spotlight in the center of the room. Ana felt the need to tiptoe into the dark room, even though everyone including her stampeded toward the light. Standing at the front was a tall, old man holding a clipboard that looked too small for his large hands.

"Everyone! Step forward please!"

The crowd stepped forward in unison.

"Who wants to get that damn chip out of your heads?"

The crowd cheered.

"Who wants to show the government who's really in charge?"

The crowd stomped their feet, shaking the platform of the building.

"For the next two days, we riot! Females, follow my staff to the right. Males, to the left."

Ana looked over at the staff dressed in suits and followed aimlessly to the right of the room.

"Last names! Follow the path of your last name!"

Ana looked at the signs above and entered the path that read 'H-L'.

The path was narrow, but the line was well-organized and in sync. At the end of the path were three chambers. Three people entered through the doors, and light illuminated their shadows through the nearly transparent doors. Ana watched their figures as a shadow of two beams approached each side of their heads. Sparks spewed from the chambers as the beams drilled into the skulls. A deafening tone echoed the room, competing with the high-pitched screams from the women in the chambers.

Those in line stared in horror, struggling to scream. Some managed to run past the proctors. When they did, an electric shot exploded from their brains, and they dropped to the ground, unconscious.

Those who accepted their fate and stayed silent entered the narrow room, expecting the unknown. Ana was one of those people.

That's why the pair was burning. They went against what they were programmed to do.

She gazed at the mass of bodies by her feet. Men in suits collected them, and before she knew it, her turn to enter the room approached.

A young woman stood next to her, waiting for the chambers to be cleared. The two looked similar in age—in their early twenties. They shared a look, but neither dared to speak.

Ana entered the room and faced the door. A screen illuminated with the words, "Riot Rat #33." A countdown from ten appeared and she could sense the two drills approach her head. She shut her eyes as the shrill vibrations blared through her eardrums. An excruciating pain ensued; a million migraines and a million electrocutions—all at once. She gritted her teeth and clenched her jaw, feeling the newly formed holes on the sides of her head, and the blood draining out of her brain. Ana opened her eyes only to be met with overpowering dizziness, causing her knees to buckle. The last thing she saw were the words, "Riot Rat #33."

Ana awoke to a blinding light. Doctors hovered over her.

"Welcome back Ana, and congratulations."

"Congratulations for what?"

"For surviving, for passing experiment #1 as a riot rat, and becoming a leader for this nation."

Ana took a deep breath. She felt empty but liberated. Her hand automatically went to her head and was met with a wet bandage.

"We took your chip out," the doctor explained, smiling fondly.

"What?" Ana felt like a different person; she no longer felt lightheaded. "What do you mean I'm going to be a leader of the nation?"

The doctors shared a look. "You, along with fifty others have been chosen as the strongest people of our nation. Despite a chip that controls your thoughts since your birth, you have executed a great form of control and intelligence that is needed to lead this country. You've been amazing riot rats for our experiment, and we'd like to reward you with high positions of your country."

"And what about our leaders now...what about President Kinley?" Ana heard of President Kinley in school, but no citizen had ever seen neither him nor his team.

"He was the man who greeted you into this building. As you may have noticed, he has grown old. In fact, we've all grown old. Our chosen citizens form a wide range of professions—doctors, scientists, governors...president. And the former team is passing their role to this next generation. You are a part of this generation." The doctor smiled brightly, and the rest of the doctors nodded.

Ana wasn't as shocked as she expected. Of course, there had to be a secret team without chips in their head, controlling the citizens who did. Of course, this team would have to grow old. Without the chip in her head, Ana understood. She stared at the doctor. "And my role is…"

"Doctor, like us. We are going to train you, and your first job will start tomorrow."

"But I've never had experience with—"

"We operated on your brain already. We took the chip out but inserted a particular card that will allow you to understand our type of medicine in less than a day. Don't worry, that's all that we controlled." He chuckled.

After ten videos and lists of notes, Ana was ready to perform her first operation.

"Alright, Ana. Your first patient—this is a special moment." The doctor approached Ana with a crying newborn in his arms. The baby screamed uncontrollably and as the doctor set her down on the table, Ana realized where the babies went to after they were born. Not a ward in the hospital—but to Operation Unchipped.

Ana's hand shook. This baby would have to experience the same manipulation and control as she did, and though that was her thought, something stopped her from voicing this opinion to the doctor. Ana held the drill, with the chip attached at the tip. As she turned it on, a loud buzz and a shock of electricity waved through the tool.

As the drill approached the baby's head, a migraine shocked Ana's brain.

"Resist, Ana, resist." The doctor repeated, staring at Ana intensely.

A cry echoed the room, but it wasn't from the baby. Tears streamed down Ana's face as the drill grazed the baby's head.

"It'll get better as you have more experience," the doctor whispered, patting Ana's shoulder, "You're being a wonderful Riot Rat."

Riot Rat. Ana turned off the drill and massaged her temples. The word illuminated in her mind as she shut her eyes, and the letters began to separate and spin. *R I O T R A T.* The familiar shock jolted through her brain. She winced. "You said you took the chip ou—"

The drill dropped to the ground and so did Ana.

"Put her with the rest of them," the doctor said, his smile gone.

T R A I T O R

DYSTOPIA

by Vivian Tang

Awarded the blossoms of snapdragons and content
The purity of the land of which I called "me"
Was nothing more than a façade, my imagination

Of hopes and dreams of becoming something more
From the fruits of life to the barrels of pain
Everything I saw were visions of my desires

With nights as dark as Hell
And days as golden as the Sun
I was stuck in Limbo with no way out

This was the universe that I created for "me"
Succumbed by its darkened veil
With only a ray of light seeping through

A utopia where hearts can be one;
A place where thoughts could be relinquished
But when all is done, these feelings rip apart

Burning passions as a metaphor
Sins without any ropes
Out of reach with what's true individuality

I have fallen deep into the Rabbit Hole
Somewhere I can no longer recall the true "me"
A realm of my own creation has taken over reality.

ON A SUMMER'S DAY

by Hiep Do

I think too much about the past
About things never meant to last.
I miss dearly summer days,
Running and smiling on the beach.
I miss dearly chilled afternoons,
Walking streets full of fallen leaves.
I miss dearly cold winter mornings,
Waking up with my hopes still brewing.
But I learn what is always true about the past
Those things were never meant to last.

Listening to the sound of summer's life,
Anticipating cold bitterness
Of the long winter's strife.
The heart will soon be freezing
Sing and dance at the moment fleeting.
I hear somewhere the call of youth,
Crying and waiting to be soothed.
So I stand up
And start to run
Into the warmth
Of the blazing sun.

Not long ago
The sun still shone,
Now conquered
By the light of stars.
No brighter here,
Than the sun who must yield
To the natural cycle of beyond

Once again I am here
Left with this feeling
Not of love or of joy
Nor of sadness or pain
Just a little sense of loneliness
In this vast world of man.

SIREN AND THE SEA

by Vivian Tang

RESTING UPON THE ROCKY shores, the siren softly sang her alluring melody. The song echoed throughout the beach, begging to be noticed by someone. An old man made his way down to the shore, searching for shells. Nothing in particular caught his eye. He picked up big shells. He picked up small shells. He picked up all kinds of shells. He lifted some up to his ear and heard the ocean. In others, he could hear the sound of falling sand.

Exploring further into the rocky shores, he noticed a feminine figure out on the rocks, staring at him. She begged out with her melodious voice, "Help me."

He looked around to see if she was speaking to anyone else, but he was alone. Something in his stomach urged him to approach her. She beckoned him closer to the water. Mesmerized, he followed her voice like a fish lured by a baited hook.

As he waded into the ocean, he began to notice how captivating she was. She was unlike any other woman he had ever seen: porcelain skin glowing while she struggled to keep her grip on the jagged rocks and rosy lips and cheeks deepening in color as she gasped for air. The tuft of messy ginger hair curled in imperfection atop her head only added to her beauty. It was as if she was Aphrodite being birthed from her shell.

As he came closer, her face gleamed with delight. She stopped fighting the angry waters around her to stay afloat. She sang a soft, soothing melody that entranced the old man, clouding his mind. He saw oceans. He saw reefs. He saw the world through her eyes. A curious yet lonely creature she was, filled with sorrow and despair. He felt her loneliness, her deep sadness.

In these vivid visions, her life, her heart, and her secrets were revealed to him. She was tired of living in the vast blue abyss called her home. She wanted to go to places, search for new things. But as always, curiosity comes with a price. While escaping from ravenous sharks, the siren had lost her pearl, the source of her magic.

Without her pearl, she knew she could no longer achieve her dream of adventure, but that didn't discourage her from trying. But nothing could stand in her way now with what she has endured.

It was a stroke of serendipity that the old man and she met and a chance for them to connect with one another. She looked down at him and smiled, thanking fate for giving her something special at that very moment.

Time was running out for the both of them. She needed to return back to the realm of the sea soon. During their last moments, she looked longingly into his eyes, admiring him once more.

"*As the days get colder, and nights get longer, why can't you come? Come faster, come closer, and listen to me,*" she began to sing. "*Follow me and I will be yours. Come faster, come closer.*"

Her words enchanted him as his desires for her grew stronger and stronger. He waded further and further from the shore toward the beautiful maiden.

And as quick as their encounter was, she wrapped an arm around his body and pulled him underwater. He did not fight the urges and simply went along with her, entranced by her song and beauty. She smiled softly, gently caressing his face as his heart slowly ceased to beat. He was soon merely a stone she dragged along with her, his limbs moving ever so slightly as the force of the water playfully pushed at his body.

She stopped swimming and turned to face the lifeless old man. She brought her lips close to his, sucking his soul out from within his heart. The siren opened her mouth and extended her tongue as she plucked the shimmering peach colored pearl off it. She released the corpse, letting the body sink to the bottom of the ocean. She turned her attention back to her palm and admired her new pearl, examining it at every angle.

"*Life comes and goes, with all the hopelessness of living. But you will be safe with me for eternity. So, come faster. Come closer.*" The siren smirked and put the pearl back into her mouth. She swam away into the depths of the ocean with the "old man" to find her collection of souls gathered from victims that had fallen prey to her.

SCULTUM

by Kelly Ho

I should have known better
Than to let my heart lead me to you
Allowing your words to melt me
I'm the only fool in this game
Falling into the memories built
Knowing better than anyone
The lies that hide behind
April Fools, you etched in my head
Now what else can I do
Stained by this love
An addiction I can't help
So stop speaking
I don't want to hear your truth
Let me keep this fluttering feeling
You and I should just fall
Into these melting recollections
Let them take us back
No, I don't want to understand
These lies now spelling truth
Your cold eyes now avoid mine
But it doesn't matter
This feeling continues
So don't let me go
Let me relive this pain
I don't care if I'm a fool

COLORS

by Phuong Traceyle

Nature represents us.
Roses splashed in red
With love or madness.
The sky tinted blue
Full of serenity and silence.
Orchids dazzled in purple
Mystery along with radiance.
Nature reflects us.

NATURE

Bee
Small, striped
Buzzing, zig-zagging, working
Nectar, flowers, pollination, honey
Fluttering, migrating, dancing
Beautiful, colorful
Butterfly

LACRIMOSA

by Jacqueline Truong

Oh moon-drunken monster,
sing your wretched melody
Bring me back to life;
wake me from my reverie

It cries its cacophony of
curling thorns and claws
Of whispers of weeping angels,
without order, without law

Could this charm
be the root of corruption?
Perhaps be the cause of
carnage and destruction?

WELCOME BACK

by Iris Sanchez

We both grew up, went through so much
We go back to each other when things get rough
When did it start?
When was it that I realized when things changed?
My heart broke a little when you thought of leaving,
even if for a second.
I didn't know what I did wrong,
Why you thought I wasn't enough anymore.
When you found someone else you related to,
Someone who liked the things you liked.
I was left behind
Time and time again
Your smile was bright, but mine was a mask
And when the time came,
When she hurt your feelings and you came back,
When you opened up your eyes and realized she didn't care.

I smiled and opened my arms.
Welcome back.

THE PERFORMANCE

by Kayla Nguyen

THE VELVET CURTAINS GLIDE open and reveal the inky black stage. A light clicks to life; its blinding white beam circles around the stage illuminating the wooden floorboards.

Music eases itself into the silence. It begins with soft, delicate notes, and then rises into a crescendo. The audience members straighten their posture in their cushioned seats. They lean closer to the stage with their hungry eyes and wait.

The music stops, and the audience hears the stage creak under the weight of a woman adorned in a soft pink dress. Her white caked face and blood-red lips shine under the yellow glow, enhancing her doll-like appearance as she makes her way to the center of the stage.

The orchestra begins another song, and the ballerina lifts her arms above her head and leans forward on her toes. She glides across the stage, reaching one arm outward toward the audience before pulling it back inward as she spins. The performer draws from the twirl to leap across the stage. She sways her arms to one side and gracefully swings them over her head.

The audience applauds as she lands on her feet, lifts up on her toes, and spins once more, her movements flowing from one pose to another. At the song's conclusion, the dancer drapes her body across the wooden floor in a dramatic low bow.

The curtains drift close and a light switches on, brightening the entire theater with its golden glow.

Intermission.

A gentleman with a worn and wrinkled-face clad in a sleek black suit makes his way from his seat in the theater to the backstage. He winds his way to the orchestra pit and opens the door.

"Great job conducting the orchestra today, Fernande," he says.

"Rosetti? Our favorite theater manager," Fernande says. He pushes a case out of Rosetti's view.

Rosetti narrows his eyes, shuts the door behind him and makes his way across the sea of instruments to the conductor, Fernande, sitting at the piano. "What are you doing?"

Fernande gives him a small smile. "Nothing much, just working on a new song."

"All right, so what's in the case?"

Fernande looks at the case and places a hand over the lid. He slowly opens it and reveals a flute. "It was a gift from our theater owner Giovanni to celebrate our theater's fifty-year anniversary. Isn't that thoughtful? Did Giovanni give you a gift as well?"

"A flute…" Rosetti averts his gaze away from the instrument. "No, he didn't give me anything."

"Nothing for our beloved theater manager?" Fernande coughs. "Do you need anything?"

"No, I just wanted to compliment you and wish you good luck with the new song."

Musicians file into the orchestra pit and begin to take their seats.

"Thank you," Fernande says.

Rosetti nods. "I'll speak with you later."

He returns to the theater where he makes eye contact with a younger man. He strides over to him.

Rosetti chuckles and reaches up to adjust his tie. "Good evening, Movius." He holds out his hand.

"Hello, Rosetti," Movius nods his head subtly but ignores the outstretched hand. He glances at the crystal chandelier hanging from the ceiling embellished with shards of stained glass. "You went all out for this, didn't you?"

Rosetti drops his hand to his side. "Of course. I couldn't let your performance beat my own." His smile grows slightly wider when he sees a bitter expression flash across Movius's face.

"It is extravagant, but I wouldn't say it's better than my performance. There's still plenty of room for improvement," Movius says, "I am curious though. Did you change the song for the play?"

"Our theater owner Giovanni gave the song to me. He said it was exclusively for today."

Movius raises his eyebrows. "Giovanni gave the new song to you?" He hesitates, seeing the curtains on stage begin to open up and the light dimming. "I knew he would."

The two men sit down onto the plush seats.

"What do you mean?" Rosetti asks. He ignores the hush from the woman next to them and leans closer to Movius.

"Isn't it obvious?" Movius quietly laughs. "Giovanni would only give you a new song if I told him to. He has always favored me and the theater I manage more than you and your theater." Movius turns his attention back to the stage.

This time the ballerina is not alone. A man disguised in a black mask and cape accompanies her on stage. Perhaps he was the new hire the director had mentioned.

The man draws a flute from under his cape and lifts the instrument to his lips. He begins to play with the rest of the orchestra. The ballerina responds by dropping her hands to her sides and relaxing her tense shoulders. Her blank face tilts to the blinding lights, but her eyes refuse to blink.

The masked man removes his lips from his flute. He looks over to the ballerina and points his hand at her.

The audience gasps when the man clenches his outstretched hand into a fist, and at the same time, the woman twists backwards into a ball. The orchestra ends their piece, and a sickening *crack* instead of a note echoes throughout the theater as she falls to the ground. The man in the mask faces the crowd and lowers his body into a sweeping bow. From the sides of the theater, clouds of smoke puff out to conceal the stage behind its thick film. Confusion ensues as the audience seems unsure of whether they had seen was real or simply theatrics. They decide it must have been the latter.

One person in the audience claps, followed by more people, until the entire auditorium is filled with applause.

A woman turns to Movius. "That was beautiful. The ballerina is such a great dancer," she says, "You could tell she's full of passion."

Movius returns her a slight smile. "I can see you enjoyed this performance, Miss."

"Yes, I—"

Movius feels a hand placed on his shoulder. He glances at Rosetti. "What?"

"I don't think that was supposed to happen." Rosetti looks around and leans closer to Movius. "I need to talk to you." Rosetti bites his lip and jerks Movius closer to him. He whispers, "Meet me at the orchestra pit, please."

Rosetti stomps down through the hallways dimly lit with a scarce number of lamps hanging from the walls. "Miserable lonely twat," Rosetti mutters. He pulls back the curtains to find his ballerina in a puddle of blood, surrounded by the theater employees who are gasping in horror. He touches her shoulder. She doesn't move.

"Get back, everyone. You." Rosetti points to one of his directors. "Call the authorities. Clear the stage. Do not touch anything." Everyone scatters away.

Rosetti heads offstage and approaches the orchestra pit. He takes a few deep breaths to calm himself, opens the door, and enters the room.

Fernande is alone in the room. "Rosetti. How was the performance of the new song?"

Rosetti clenches his fist. "Our star performer, she's dead."

Fernande blinks and peers at Rosetti's stern expression. The frown painted over Fernande's face curves into a smile. His laughter fills the room. "What?" he says in a mocking tone, "Did she mysteriously fall to the floor and die?"

"No." Rosetti grits his teeth. "How could you not realize what's happened above your head onstage? The screams? The commotion? What's wrong with you? The authorities are on their way. Someone has killed her. The masked man. Who was he?" Rosetti pauses in deep thought. "Perhaps it was Giovanni."

"Giovanni?" Fernande said. "Why would the theater owner do that?"

"We've never seen him before, only spoken to him through phone and written correspondence. What if he's a criminal?"

Fernande scoffs and narrows his eyebrows. "That's way too far-fetched Rosetti. If he was a criminal, he would have been caught by now."

"Not if he doesn't show his face," Rosetti says, "and that's not all. How can you explain when someone makes a slight tweak to a set or song, they disappear the next day? Perhaps Giovanni is behind something sinister even if it's not murder. It's no longer a cruel coincidence."

"I—"

Knock knock. "That's for me," Rosetti says. He walks out the door and slams it behind him. "Movius, you're finally here." Rosetti grabs Movius's hand and pulls him down, closer to his face. "Listen closely, the ballerina's dead and I suspect Giovanni killed her—"

Movius covers Rosetti's mouth with his palm. "Are you out of your mind?"

Rosetti yanks Movius's hand away from his face. "Don't interrupt me. Someone murdered our star, and we need to find out who. She died right after the masked man finished his song. We must confront Giovanni." Rosetti paces, recounting Fernande presenting him the flute. *Why would Movius give Fernande a flute, if he doesn't play the flute?*

A shriek bounces off the walls of the hallway and the two men jump. They turn around, Rosetti wrenches the door open, and they find Fernande shriveled up on the floor.

Fernande clutches his stomach. With his mouthing hanging open, he coughs out a patch of blood. Fernande looks up at them and they gasp. Fernande's face is ghostly pale, his eyes bloodshot.

Movius runs up to Fernande, who cries out again, flailing his arms around. Movius grabs his hand, and Fernande screeches in pain. He curls up tighter on tighter on the floor, continuously twitching, until he stops moving.

Movius stares wide-eyed at the dead man. "This can't be happening." He grabs Rosetti by the shoulders. "What did you do to him? Why's he dead?"

"No, no." Rosetti shakes his head and back away. "I didn't do anything, I swear."

Movius tightens his grip around Rosetti's shoulders. He shoves Rosetti down to the floor. "Get away from me," Movius screams. "You...monster. What have you done to Fernande?"

Rosetti shakes his head. He reaches out to grab Movius's hand. "Movius listen to me. I did nothing. I'm just as shocked as you."

Movius jerks his hand away and backs away from Rosetti. "No, I knew you always had it in for Fernande. You were always suspicious of him, you monster." Movius takes one last glance at Rosetti and flees down the hallway.

Rosetti hobbles around the hallways in search for the young man. "Movius," he hollers, "please, believe me. I didn't do it."

Rosetti wanders around for a while and finally shuffles into the auditorium. It is empty now, not a person in sight. All the theater employees, dancers, and musicians had cleared the area, still awaiting the paramedics and police. "Movius? Where are you?" His voice echoes in the vacant theater and sends down a sprinkle of dust. Rosetti sneezes. He rubs his nose and looks up to see a man clinging to the chandelier. He gasps and stumbles backward.

Rosetti sighs in relief. He realizes it isn't a man, but a shadow from the crystal chandelier lights. Rosetti shakes his head. He turns around, and a masked man, the same one who killed the ballerina earlier onstage, shoves a knife through Rosetti's eye.

At the same time, unaware of what was happening in the theater, Movius returns down the hall leading to the orchestra pit. "Maybe Rosetti isn't a monster," he mumbles, "He's too old to kill anyway."

The light from the music room spills outside into the hallway. It beckons Movius closer, tempting him to take a look. Movius peeks through the doorway and gasps. There is a woman, not just any woman, but the ballerina, holding a knife. Movius falls back onto his bottom, and sits there wide-eyed.

The ballerina grabs his foot and Movius lets out a strangled cry. He attempts to crawl away, but she pulls him closer to herself and looks directly into his eyes.

"You're alive?" Movius says, "Rosetti said you were dead!"

"I'm alive." The ballerina giggles. "But you won't be." She points one of her fingers down.

Movius follows the ballerina's finger with his eyes. She points at his stomach. He looks up at her in disbelief, and she stabs him in the stomach with a knife.

THE NIGHT SKY ACTS as an ebony canvas with splashes of white specks. The young ballerina shoves her mitten-covered hands into her coat pockets. She breathes out, allowing a puff of mist to leave her mouth and enter the freezing air. She had just finished another successful performance.

Down the street, there is a lump in the snow. She narrows her eyes and moves closer. It is a man. He clutches his foot, groaning as she approaches him. She stares at him for a good minute before shaking her head.

"Are you alright?" she asks. The ballerina holds out her hand, which the man grabs onto immediately, and she hauls him up.

He dusts off the snow off his clothes before facing the woman. "Thank you," he says, "I slipped when running on the snow."

The ballerina avoids the man's stare and looks at her feet instead. She notices a glint of silver in the snow and bends down. It was a flute. "You should be more careful Fernande," she says, standing up and handing him the instrument. "You could have hurt yourself."

Fernande takes the flute. "You performed well today."

She gives him a dimpled smile. "Thank you." A frown quickly overtakes her face. "But now what? We can't continue performing. We're missing managers for both theaters."

Fernande brings his hand to his chin. "I guess it is about time we hire some new people. Rosetti and Movius were getting boring anyway."

"Boring? I thought their rivalry was quite entertaining."

"Yes, they were an interesting pair. The problem was that Rosetti nearly found out who I was, and we can't have that happening."

The ballerina nods her head, and then gasps. She jumps up and down on the balls of her feet. "I want to help you hire. What can I—"

"No," Fernande says, "I'm the boss. I'll decide on my own." He glares at her, and she lowers her head.

"Okay, Fernande . . . Or shall I say, Giovanni? What will you do if the new employees are like Rosetti? What if they find out we're criminals? That this is all a sick game?"

A large smile stretches across Fernande's face. "Then we'll end their performance."

NIGHT TIME

by Aysha Pena

I only think about it in the night time,
Always in the night time.
Just to pass time
Can't think about it for too long
Since it's so wrong,
Still remember how you'd tag along
Hang out all day long
Our bond so strong
Now everything is all gone.
You just lead me on
Making me hold on,
So in my free time
I'll just think about it in the night time.

SKY

by Jennifer Ho

No matter how much light comes in,
It is still dark
The window is my escape
From this living hell,
I try to not weep—
It will only cause more misery.

No matter how long it has been,
I still do not have a name
They only call me by pronouns
Attached with harshness,
But I will go by...
Sky—
If anyone asks.

Through the bars, the Sky
Looks rather small,
But the picture will be complete—
If I am the Sky, too.

DREAMERS

by Valerie Nguyen

I'm a dreamer day and night
But it comes alive
In my slumber.
I see it
I feel it
And I want to live it forever.
But only when night comes around
Am I allowed to truly live as a dreamer
But I can't control what happens.

I'm a dreamer
Who lives through
Love, horror, and adventures.
I can't possibly make these events
Happen in real life
Or I might actually die.

So during the nighttime
I get to dream
All these wonderful things
And truly become a dreamer
But only in my slumber.

RAIN

by Paulvina Tran

Drip drop drip drop…
God cries from Heaven
Pouring down on Earth
Humans take cover
The Sun appears,
Clouds disappear,
Humans sing,
Rain, Rain, come again
come again, another day.
A Week later,
Rain pours hard,
Drenching humans,
Making loud noises,
Drip drop drip drop…

THE EYES

by Iris Sanchez

I seek a way to help the girl on the floor
All I see are her eyes
Judgmental disgust from within.
I want to run, I want to hide
"Don't look at me" roared through my head.
Not long after, I noticed *their* eyes.
I had to stay inside.
I refused to go to stores
I began talking less
Their eyes pierced through me and
All I felt was shame.
Was I not good enough?
Am I useless?

As I began to hide myself
The more I realized
No longer can I escape my safe haven,
Nothing more than a jail cell now.
Restraining me, preventing me from escape
I'm stuck in this never ending cycle
Glued onto this path.

Only a few months back
I had realized the Hell I had created.
I built up the walls surrounding me,
No one allowed in, I can't get out.
A house with no door, no windows
Sunlight mocks me with warmth I cannot feel
The shadows in the night tap on the windows.
I hide myself in a corner, knowing no one can get in,
I hear glass shatter

My eyes open wide
How could this happen?

A hand reaches in, grabs onto the window sill
Another loud bang is heard
from all sides of the house.
I was perplexed, not knowing what to do?

These groups of girls had torn down my Hell,
Filling my darkness with warmth
My house was broken now
And all I could say to them was
Thank you all.

SPICE

by Ngoc Pham

SAVINO ACARDI HAD ALWAYS found it difficult to express his feelings to his best friend, Antonio. Perhaps it was too far of a stretch to call him a friend. Bitterness remained in Savino's heart, as he remembered that Antonio had abruptly left without a word ten years ago to go to culinary school and establish a new career. It was undeniable that Antonio had the skills to become successful.

When Antonio reappeared into Savino's life as abruptly as he left, begging for Savino to join him in managing his new restaurant "Il Pomodoro," Savino had agreed. Why had he agreed? He couldn't explain it to himself or anyone else.

Savino's sister, Fae, was irritated to learn of Antonio's return. She was even more displeased to hear her brother had welcomed him back so easily and agreed to co-manage the new restaurant. However, Savino, although still bitter, seemed happier. It was a strange mix, but Fae figured her brother was getting what he had been wanting—an explanation.

Fae brushed aside her own feelings of anger, concluding that she would help the two of them reconcile, if not force Savino to break his bad habit, the wall of dishonesty that had built up over the years with which she attributed to the pain of his best friend's abandonment.

SAVINO ACCARDI WANTED THE restaurant to be named "Venezia," or Venice, but Antonio insisted on "Il Pomodoro," "The Tomato," claiming it would attract more customers. Regardless of the name, Savino was impressed by the restaurant's unique decor, a blending of modern and ancient architectural design. The furniture, built with the finest South American blood wood, glowed when the sun struck the varnished surfaces. The many portraits and landscapes hung on the wall paired with jazz music humming from the speakers gave it a welcoming atmosphere.

Savino released the tension he hadn't known he'd been holding from his shoulders, inhaling and exhaling as the low hum of the air conditioning filled his ears.

"Savino, you're finally here," Antonio called out from the kitchen. "Come try this new dish."

Savino strode into the kitchen. A strong aroma of spices hit him, causing him to sneeze.

Antonio approached him, holding a spoon containing pork and a bit of sauce up to Savino's mouth. The freshly cooked sauce had hints of roasted tomato and garlic paired with chopped onions and pork; the fragrant and savory smell of herbs and spices mixed in the broth lingered in the air, making his mouth water.

"This kitchen reeks so strongly of spice; how do you even cook in this environment—" Savino tried to tug open a window, only to have food shoved in his mouth, making him gag as drops of tears pricked in the corners of his eyes.

"So, how is it?" Antonio clasped his hands together as his eyes sparkled, watching him chew.

Savino grabbed a glass of water, gulping down the liquid. "It tastes like the tears I'm drinking from this very cup."

"Again?" His eyes drooped along with his shoulders and his lips curved into a frown. He sat on the stool, staring at the recipe of the special dish on the glass table. There were plenty of "X" marks scattered over the page on the number of tablespoons required for each spice. He sighed looking at everything circled on the recipe. He had underestimated the difficulty of this dish.

"Look—" Savino felt a vibration in his back pocket. He whipped out his phone, frowning at the name across the screen. "Hold up." Savino walked out of the restaurant and placed the phone against his ear. From the other side of the line, he heard something shatter as things clattered against each other. "What do you want, Fae?"

"Savino, can you go to the store and buy me hairspray?"

"I'm busy right now. What's the urgency?" Savino's eyes drifted to the food stains and crumbs littering the countertops. Antonio really needed to tidy up. "Why don't you just go get it yourself?"

"What's more important than helping out your loving sister?"

He groaned, imagining her wiggling her eyebrows with a wide grin plastered on her face.

"Come on, I really need it right now. I'm going to a party later, and I can't leave the house since I need to find a nice dress," she pleaded. "Besides you're the one who used up the rest of the hairspray."

"Fine." Savino rolled his eyes. "You owe me though."

She chuckled. "Love you!"

Savino crinkled his nose at the smooching noises his sister was making. "Gross." He hung up, turned around and saw Antonio leaning against the door frame with his arms crossed.

"Guess I have to start over with the sauce." Antonio kicked the corner. "Again."

SAVINO MADE HIS WAY to the flashily decorated bedroom door, a sloppy plaque hung over its surface, reading "Fae" in large bubble letters. He walked inside and saw Fae in the middle of putting on her eye shadow. Her cosmetics were sprawled across the table's surface. One lipstick tube rolled off the surface and a few others followed suit, creating a series of clatters as they met the floor. He placed the hairspray bottle on the now empty space on the counter.

"So, how did it go with Antonio? You said you were *busy*." Fae smirked while fumbling through her drawers.

"You don't even know. It was a mess," Savino said. He plopped himself into Fae's bed. "The sauce is a disaster."

"What? Did you criticize him again?" She glanced at him, holding her eyeliner to her lashes.

"I did. I told him that his food was disgusting. I mean the new dish, his house special, was actually amazing. It was well made. The meat was so tender it melted in my mouth. The sauce fit so well with the meat and fresh vegetables. How could I end up telling him that it was too salty? I don't even know what I'm talking about, everything was so well-balanced."

Beep!

Savino paused as his sister slipped her phone back into her pocket. "What was that?"

"My friend texted me," she said. "The party waits for no one. She was worried I'd be late, that's all."

Savino raised his eyebrows. Knowing Fae, it was more than that. She was hiding something.

Fae spoke, pulling him away from his own suspicions. "Where's the hairspray?"

"It's on the table." He pointed. "Right in front of you."

Fae made no notion of moving and merely stared at him, an unreadable expression worn upon her features.

"Why are you looking at me like that?" he asked.

After a moment, a ridiculous smile crept onto her face.

Savino shook his head. "Whatever. I'm going to my room."

Fae giggled. "Thanks for the hairspray."

Savino lay onto his bed and inhaled deeply. Maybe a nap would help after today. He rolled onto his pillow, groaning into the fabric. He had made the same mistake, again, lying to Antonio. He was drifting off to sleep when his phone vibrated. He grumbled and reached over to his bedside table for the device. It was Antonio.

"Hello," he said flatly, his voice hoarse.

"Sorry, did I wake you up?"

"Obviously." Savino grumbled. "What do you need?"

"You know." Antonio hesitated. "I heard some stuff from your sister." Another pause. "She sent me an audio."

Savino's heart started to beat faster. He remembered that smile on her face. She *could*. She could, and she *did*. He knew he shouldn't have trusted her.

"It's about your food, huh?" Savino closed his eyes. "Sorry I lied."

"I'm glad to hear your honest thoughts. It's been so long since you've said something positive about my food."

"Yeah, it's been a while," he agreed. Savino looked at the photo on his phone screen, a childhood picture of the two of them hanging out at the beach. "Hey Antonio?" he said. The words bubbled in his throat. He had waited for too long, and now it would overflow—his thoughts, his feelings. But that didn't matter; he only wanted to get them across. No matter how awkward, how strange it would sound, he didn't care, he'd say it.

"Yes?"

"I like, no, I *love* your cooking. I really mean it. The passion you put into each dish is unbelievable, the flavors are amazing." Savino inhaled. "What I'm trying to say is," he began, "Never let anyone, even me, stop you from cooking. You're an amazing chef, not only for the quality of your food, but also because of your love for cooking."

The other line fell silent.

"Thank you for telling me that, I really needed it," Antonio said. "I know what this is about. I'm sorry I was a jerk. I shouldn't have lied to you and disappeared for so long. We've got a long history together. I know I never apologized. Do me a favor though. Promise me next time you'll just tell me straight up if you like my dish or not."

"Yeah," Savino said with a laugh, "We'll both be honest."

WHEN THE SUN FALLS

by Tiffany Le

It happened once more
The shining sky affirms divine wrath
Upon those below

It won't stop
It bashes me
Shaping me into a part of its universe
Making me a meteor, a seed

Its scornful ego inflated
I have been bashed so long
I no longer feel degraded

Must it be so hard, the sun says
You're always so gray
Look up, you'll feel it too
My light upon your worthless, helpless face
I will rid of your old self, without a trace.

I, who tried so hard—always overshadowed
By those whose flowers blossom
And I, alone, left to wilt, forgotten

My friends blossom, my siblings, my cousins, too
I stand by their side, so close, so near
Conceal my envy through smiles and laughter
But this envy has become too much.

Some of the people—lilies, so pure
But nothing more than a facade,
Something so vile, even others can't endure

You see it, too, right? A girl says to me
She is dull yet bright, her hair as dark as night
Looking me directly in the eye, with her cold eyes

I don't think you realize, she continues
That they, too, have obeyed that red star
Forgetting their old selves, without a trace

Behind her, the red radiant sun falls
Oozing crimson, screeches heard from all

You see it now, it spews out lies,
Join me, she says, with the sun, do not rise
Let yourself flower, blossom at your own pace
Join me, she says once more, and let us run far.

YOU

by Krista Phanpraphou

Appearances does not matter
Believe in who you are
Chase off those negative doubts
Daring as you can be
Emphasize your natural beauty
Fight for what you believe
Grasp onto hope
Haters gonna hate
I don't really care because,
Jokes on you
Kiss yourself in the mirror
Look at yourself carefully
Moments of self-love is important
Not until you become overly confident
Optimistic is key
Perseverance also stands as beauty
Quietness is peace
Rowdiness is not
Sadness, Sorrow, and Satan
Trust no devil
Understand your own desires and feelings
Violence must not corrupt your innocence
Wash away others and self-criticisms
Xenial as you can be with strangers
Your communicative abilities matter
Zippy to others, and being zippy to your own self

ALONE

by Bethanie Luu

ALONE. EVEN WHEN IN a room bursting at its seams with people, Hyunshik felt alone. He never knew why. He spent his entire life searching for someone who would allow him to experience the warm feeling of another but to no avail. Through all the years he lived, he felt only cold and isolation. Until he met *him*.

Upon merely setting his eyes on the other, Hyunshik could feel the first sparks of a fire igniting within his heart, slight warmth emanating throughout his body. It was then that he knew—Kyungsoo was special.

HYUNSHIK SHIVERED AS HE stepped out onto the roof of the abandoned parking structure, hugging his faded yellow sketchbook closer to his body, his brown hair parted to a side. A lone figure lay on the asphalt ahead of him, an arm stretched upward into the air as if trying to scoop the twinkling stars from the midnight sky.

Kyungsoo.

A gust of wind blew over the roof, ruffling Kyungsoo's dyed baby blue locks and rustling the pages of the black leather-bound sketchbook beside him. Hyunshik took another step forward, an unusual but comforting feeling of warmth beginning to pool within him. His foot hit a discarded can, sending it across the broken gravel with a rattle. He flinched as he silently prayed the other male wouldn't notice.

Kyungsoo allowed his outstretched hand to fall back onto his stomach, his eyes still locked on the sky. "What do you want from me?"

Hyunshik's breath hitched in his throat. "Nothing." His face flushed as Kyungsoo turned his head to face him, his expression unreadable. "Really."

"Everyone wants something."

Hyunshik stumbled forward and sat next to Kyungsoo. There was a heavy silence for a few moments before Hyunshik spoke. "Aren't you cold?"

Kyungsoo's eyes widened from underneath his blue hair before he recomposed himself to hide his shock. "A bit. But I'm a little warmer now that you're here."

Hyunshik smiled and crossed his outstretched legs. He watched Kyungsoo press his hands to the rough ground, pushing himself upward into a sitting position. He pondered upon what had been said and turned away. "Wait. Do you mean you can feel it too?" Hyunshik paused. "The warmth?"

Kyungsoo opened his mouth, about to speak, but no sound came out. He only stared at Hyunshik, his eyes searching the younger's face. He finally let out a nervous dry laugh, his gaze flitting down to his lap. "What do you mean?"

Hyunshik pressed his lips together into a thin line. "How many times?"

"I-" Kyungsoo sighed and tilted his head upward to look at the stars. "I don't remember. I lost count years ago. Too much pain."

"I'm sorry."

Kyungsoo smiled at Hyunshik, his eyes fighting back the waves of painful memories and tears he tried to suppress over the course of thousands of years. "Don't be." He pursed his lips. "How about you? How many times? How many lives?"

"I've had seven." Hyunshik ran his thumb over the faded yellow cover of his sketchbook. "The first time it started for me, I was a soldier fighting for my country. I remember a bullet going through my head, and when I woke up, I didn't know where I was."

"It's painful. It's a curse."

***

"Have you ever tried killing yourself before?" Hyunshik took a small sip out of his cup.

The soft clinking of cups against plates and soft idle chatter sounded throughout the coffee shop as a soft golden light pooled in through the windows, and the air smelt of coffee beans and sweet treats.

Hyunshik's long fingers were wrapped around a warm cup of coffee. Kyungsoo's coffee cup sat on the table, cold and untouched.

Kyungsoo replied, "I have, plenty of times. But it doesn't do any good. Just spits you right back into another life."

"Oh."

He reached out a pale hand, fingers gently lacing themselves around the white coffee mug. "I told you. It's a curse."

The next day, at Kyungsoo's house, Hyunshik pondered over Kyungsoo's words. It's a curse.

The door before him opened, revealing Kyungsoo. He beckoned Hyunshik inside. No words were exchanged until Hyunshik looked at one of the walls. It was covered in paintings of different colors and depictions, each one seeming to have its own story.

"Each one represents my lifetimes and dreams," Kyungsoo said. "See that one with the princess?"

In the image, a young woman in a magnificent royal blue gown knelt before a faceless man as if she were begging him for mercy.

"That was my first time," Kyungsoo said.

Hyunshik's gaze didn't leave the wall. "So you were originally female?"

"I don't know. But it was cold when I woke up again."

They were both silent, even when the Hyunshik felt smaller fingers tangle themselves between his. And so they stood like that for a while in silence, their hands intertwined as they stared at Kyungsoo's painted stories, his lifetimes. For a moment, Hyunshik felt like he wanted to stay like that forever.

***

"How long do you think before it takes us away?" asked Hyunshik. He watched Kyungsoo shovel eggs into his mouth.

They were sitting across from each other in Kyungsoo's kitchen, their feet touching beneath the table. Kyungsoo's blue hair was messy from sleep, his eyes puffy as he slumped in his oversized sleeping clothes.

Hyunshik didn't care. Even if Kyungsoo had a crumb on his chin, he was still breathtaking.

"I don't know." Kyungsoo made eye contact with him as he lazily cocked his head to the side. "It could be later or tomorrow or even tonight."

Hyunshik nodded. He had an uneasy feeling sloshing around in his stomach. "I want to stay."

Kyungsoo didn't say anything.

***

The two of them lay in Kyungsoo's bed in silence. Kyungsoo's back faced Hyunshik.

Hyunshik was about to drift into a deep slumber when the other's drawling voice pulled him back. "Who's Byungchul?"

Hyunshik stayed silent.

"Hyunshik, who's Byungchul?" Kyungsoo repeated.

Byungchul. Hyunshik had heard that name before. Byungchul. Byungchul.

Hyunshik remembered. Byungchul was the boy who fell in love with him, or rather with Eunhee, Hyunshik's identify from a previous life, Hyunshik's fourth life.

How did Kyungsoo know Byungchul's name?

"Byungchul?" Hyunshik said.

"Yes, Byungchul."

Hyunshik didn't know how to answer. He heard the flipping of pages and caught sight of faded lemon yellow. His sketchbook. "He's nothing."

The bed shifted and creaked as Kyungsoo turned to face him. "So when I disappear, will I become nothing too?"

Weeks passed with no sign of Kyungsoo. Hyunshik was alone again as he seemed destined to be. But for some reason, he simply could not stop thinking of *him*. Byungchul was the boy Eunhee loved, but Hyunshik wasn't Eunhee. At least, not anymore. Right now, Hyunshik was Hyunshik.

Hyunshik missed the way Kyungsoo's face brightened up when he smiled. He missed the chimes of Kyungsoo's laughter. He missed how soft Kyungsoo's hair was when he ran his fingers through it. He missed how warm he felt with Kyungsoo. Hyunshik missed Kyungsoo and didn't want to lose him.

***

"I'm sorry."

"I'm sorry too," Hyunshik said, exhaling as he felt his walls of guilt and emptiness fall.

"It's okay." Kyungsoo stood before him in his living room, bags beneath his bloodshot eyes.

Hyunshik admitted he hadn't been faring well, either. He managed to crack a small smile. "I want to stay."

"Me too."

And with that, Hyunshik pushed his lips onto the former's chapped ones. He didn't know why he was kissing him. He only knew that they both felt warm.

Kyungsoo was a tattered mess but a beautiful one all the same. Hyunshik was in love with him.

***

Cold.

Something was odd, and he could feel it. That was what woke Hyunshik up. He wished he hadn't opened his eyes. The space beside him was empty.

Where are you?

Hyunshik's heart began to hammer and race within his chest. He stumbled through the hallway and into the kitchen. Empty. He shoved the bathroom door open. Empty. He looked in the tub, under the couch and under the bed. Empty.

He kept saying the same words in his head and under his breath.

"Stay. Stay, stay, stay, stay, stay."

But the house was quiet. He couldn't hear Kyungsoo breathing. The only signs that he was ever really there was the fading warmth within him and clothes left strewn on the floor.

"No! Give us more time!"

A piece of yellowed paper torn out of a sketchbook lay on the white sheets of Kyungsoo's side of the bed. Hyunshik stared at it before reaching out a trembling hand to pick it up. His eyes passed over what was written onto it. Kyungsoo's last words or rather, a single word.

Hyunshik hugged it to his chest, collapsing to his knees as wretched sobs escaped in cries and wails from his throat.

They took you away, didn't they?

COLD AND ALONE. THE woman always accepted them for what they were, only knowing that she used to know what warmth was. She remembered that in a past life as a man, she met another who loved her. And he was like her.

But now all of that was lost. She only had her faded lemon sketchbook with her to keep her company along with the short snippets of memories she retained from all the lifetimes she had. She ran her thumb over its textured leather spine, shivering as a slight wind blew her hair in her face. She dropped the sketchbook as she reached up to brush aside the strands.

But when she looked down to pick it up, it opened to reveal a yellowed page, a page that didn't belong in there, a name scribbled on the ripped corner.

Kyungsoo.

Un-

by Kelly Ho

Like a habit, I hold onto you
Pretending we're okay
Smile, I tell myself
I still love you
So again I kiss you
You are the sun in my sky
Everything's the same
We're still in love
Nothing has changed
As I put on a smile
You still make me weak
My heart still flutters

A VISION IN LIFE

by Vy Ngo

The same routine
It wore you down
Until you drowned
In the fact that you were achieving nothing
By doing everything.

I've heard, from a wise, old man
"Don't follow your dreams."
The path in life can take you anywhere
But once you got there, was it worth it?

Life fired opportunities at you
But you chose to put up a shield.
The brain that you wield, in your vulnerable skull
Why, then, was life so dull?

The decision you made, was it correct?
You stumbled blindly into life
Oblivious to what's up ahead.
You thought you'd figured it out
But the blind can only imagine.

THE DARKNESS
by Aimee Geck

Humans are like glass
We break but can't repair
If it were easy, we would pass
This inevitable despair
The Darkness is inescapable
Like an eternity of night
Once caught, you're entrapped in a gape
Doomed to suffer eternal melancholy

REBEL
by Jennifer Ho

They wonder why I am so… rebellious
It is because they never offered me a chance to be myself

The many years of them bickering at my mistakes
Shaming my appearance, friends, and decisions

How I wanted them to cease their obstructive words
But they kept spewing them out like an active volcano

Destroying the already damaged pathways to my heart
Permanently.

FLASH MY WINGS

by Christine Vu

COMPARED TO THE FLOWER bushes sprinkled about the village, the fairies are more colorful. Goldsprig observed this as she looked out the carriage window, watching everybody going about their casual days. She folded her wings and tucked them under her tulip cloak. She had chosen a plain taxi, hoping to go about incognito this day. It was windy—fairies wouldn't fly in this weather, unless they had large or strong wings. Either way, most fairies preferred to walk or call cabs.

Goldsprig thanked the cab driver and opened up the door, slowly stepping out. She slipped on sunglasses and walked inside a café, eyeing a nectar frappe and raspberry tart. So far, so good. Now, don't mess up.

Her drink took forever to arrive. Goldsprig fidgeted in her place as she checked the clock every few seconds.

"Nectar frappe with marigold morsels and snow?"

Goldsprig leapt in her spot. Yes, finally. She picked up her drink and tart before finding a seat in the back of the room. There were no windows, thus, dim lighting—perfect for hiding. Her sneakers tapped their way towards the seat, but she froze a couple of steps away. Somebody was already sitting there. They took the one hiding spot. Goldsprig swallowed, her grip tightening on her drink. What to do now?

She turned around and headed towards the door while finishing her tart, quickly tossing the wrapper before rushing outside. With one hand clutching her cloak, she pushed through the wind to the road—she'd have to wait for the gust to pass before hailing a cab.

Just as she lifted her hand, another gust of wind blew by, opening her cloak with it. Her transparent wings, now exposed, caught the sunlight and flashed a rainbow gloss. Its faint veins, like those found on leaves, glistened brighter than the wings themselves. That sort of shine could be attracting eyes any second now, and Goldsprig knew that.

She attempted to grab her cloak, but moving around caused it to loosen and detach. Her eyes widened as the cloak flew away and her dragonfly wings unfurled, dorsal and ventral wings pointing away from each other.

Gasps escaped from everybody's lips. Goldsprig's breathing hitched and her eyes widened.

"Look, it's her! Goldsprig is here," somebody exclaimed.

"I can't believe she's right in front of me."

"She looks even more beautiful in person."

Goldsprig noticed her cloak caught onto a fence. She ran up to it, but fairies started crowding around her. They flashed their cameras as she covered her face with her hands and tucked her wings down. She pushed past the circling fairies and reached for the cloak, but within the struggle somebody got to it before her.

"Her cloak," that fairy announced, "I have her cloak." That kind of proclamation caused a tussle over the cloak.

Goldsprig pulled back her hand. She could feel somebody touching her, another breathing down on her wings. Her eyes darted around. She ran a hand through her rosemary-green hair. She had to get away.

She pushed herself past the camera flashes and reached for her cloak. Trying to pull away from the crowd while tugging for her cloak out of a fairy's clutch caused it to tear at the bottom. With so many fairies crowding around her, Goldsprig scratched her arm and dropped her drink as she flew away. Her wings beating against the wind drowned out the camera clicks.

***

Bam! Orchidvey lifted his head to the door. Looks like somebody's back.

"Orchid, it happened again," Goldsprig cried out, lifting up her marred cloak.

Orchidvey cocked his head. "Well, you should have gone with the maple. Stiffer material and all that. Don't worry, I'll stitch that up in a week," he said with a shrug. He turned back to his magazine, flipping a page.

Goldsprig shook her head. "No, I'm not talking about that," she replied with her hands flying about, "I was talking about those...those—"

"—The paparazzi again?" Orchidvey leaned back in his chair.

"Yes."

"You say that every time you go out. Just get secret service or something. Your parents do that."

Goldsprig placed a hand on her hip. "They do that when they're going somewhere formal and important. I just want a casual, normal day like everybody else."

"My days are never normal," Orchidvey replied. "I get to work with you."

"Not just work with me. You're my best friend," Goldsprig said.

Orchidvey smiled.

Goldsprig dropped her head and breathed out a laugh. She shook her head and threw the tulip cloak at his arms.

132

"I'm right, huh? Nobody else is as lucky as I am. I see your clothes, your photo-shoots, the works. Front row seat, free of charge. I didn't even ask for it," Orchidvey said as he folded up the cloak.

"And you're not a celebrity, Orchid?" Goldsprig sneered. She took off her shoes, left them in the mud room, and flew past Orchidvey's desk.

Orchidvey pushed himself out of his seat and flew after her. "Come on— your mom, Oakfroth, has a lot of fans, and so does your dad, Sparkrain. People lost it when they found out the two got married and had a child. Can you believe it? Two different races," he said. His purple flower wings fluttered slower than Goldsprig's Crystal-Dragonfly wings.

Goldsprig stopped mid-flight, causing Orchidvey to almost bump into her. "I'm famous because of how I look. You don't see Dragonflies with paler lines and flashing colors. You don't see any fairies with their wings looking like a diagonal cross. Not around here."

"Actually, I have."

Goldsprig turned around and narrowed her eyes. Orchidvey flew backwards so not to get scratched by her wings.

"You're being serious, Orchid?" Goldsprig asked.

"Want me to prove it?" Orchidvey replied. The two maintained eye contact for a minute. "I'll take you a party," he added.

GOLDSPRING FROWNED AT HER reflection in the illuminated vanity mirror. She and Orchidvey had agreed to meet at his house under the pretenses of having sleepover, but he had actually arranged for a night away from town, far away, but still close enough to return home unnoticed before morning.

So far, Goldsprig had never succeeded in fleeing. She always got caught by the cameras.

Goldsprig wiped her hands on her pants before lifting up a duffle bag. After double checking the contents, she flew out to her waiting parents in the living room.

"See you in the morning," said her mom, Oakfroth, with a hug.

"Have fun," added her dad, Sparkrain, with a tighter hug.

Goldsprig smiled weakly as she said her goodbyes and flew outside the house. She hadn't gotten far but already felt she'd committed a crime. Her wings fluttered faster than usual, and she arrived at Orchidvey's house earlier than she expected. She landed, but her wings continued to vibrate. She knocked on the door, and was soon after met by Orchidvey's mother, Mrs. Cedarzhu, a friend of Goldsprig's parents.

"Ah, good evening, Miss Goldsprig," Mrs. Cedarzhu greeted as she opened the door. "Orchid is in the kitchen making a snack."

"Good evening, Mrs. Cedarzhu." Goldsprig stepped inside with a smile. She flew to the kitchen and caught sight of the large purple wings.

Orchidvey smiled. "Hello there. I'm making pollen cakes. Do you want any?"

Orchidvey never made anything from scratch. Rather, he combined pre-packaged foods together and calls the new creation a cake.

"Sure. I'll have it with snow if you have any," Goldsprig replied.

Orchidvey held up a tray with cakes and flew out of the kitchen. "Yes, they're in the fridge. I'm bringing this to my room."

Goldsprig pulled out a bowl of snow from the fridge and followed after him. She dropped her duffle bag onto the floor, next to the bed. She set the bowl down on his vanity table, next to the tray and prepared herself a snack for the time being.

Orchidvey shut his bedroom door. "Alright. So if we're going to sneak out, we need to turn on the TV in the living room and pretend we're watching a movie. We'll be doing that when my parents are asleep. They sleep early."

Goldsprig nodded, chewing on her cake and his plan.

"Before we do so, we have to do something about your look. Disguise and all," he added with a gesture to her figure.

She looked down at herself and her plain pajamas.

Orchidvey zipped towards the vanity table, pushing aside Goldsprig, and spread out up his makeup set. He flung open his closet and pulled out an assortment of clothes and tossed them onto his bed. He unzipped Goldsprig's duffle bag and pulled out some clothes, much to the dismay of his best friend. He rushed over to a spare wardrobe to open the doors, but stopped short.

Goldsprig flew over to his side. She gasped, hands covering her mouth.

Inside the wardrobe were many outfits covered in a transparent film-like material. Some Goldsprig had seen before and some she had never laid eyes on until now. The moment ended too soon, because Orchidvey fanned out his wings and shut the doors.

"You weren't supposed to see that," he said.

"Are those for my next photo-shoot?"

"Yes." He opened the doors again, slower this time, and selected the outfits Goldsprig had worn before. "Don't wear anything too obvious. You want to blend in? Dress like the crowd, not like the magazine. And make it practical."

He turned around and scanned the options. He smiled as he selected an eggshell blue turtleneck, matching trousers, and a ballet pink jumper.

"Here, put these on. I'll prepare the rest," he said, throwing them to Goldsprig's direction. She barely succeeded in catching them. "And change in here. My parents will know what we're doing if you change in the washroom."

She flew over to a corner of the room and fanned out her wings. When peeking behind her, Goldsprig noticed Orchidvey walking on the floor with his wings also fanned out, she cursed at his large flower wings under breath.

How lucky he was. Those wings were obviously better at hiding oneself than her not-opaque Crystal-Dragonfly wings.

Despite how much Orchidvey respected her privacy, Goldsprig changed out of her pajamas as quickly as she could. She turned around and noticed her best friend still searching through the options.

"Orchid, it'll be cold outside. I'll need a cloak."

"Like I said, Maple. Sit here and pick any of these scarves."

Goldsprig seated herself in front of his vanity, the chair turned away from the mirror.

"Good thing it's a long-sleeve. Makes my work easier," Orchidvey commented as he whipped out a makeup brush. He began dabbing at the sea foam color of his makeup palette.

He brushed over any of her exposed skin, taking care not to get any color on her hair or clothes. "I was thinking of doing your wings but we don't have time for that. Just make sure to fold, okay Spree?"

Goldsprig had selected a spider silk scarf and her stylist began wrapping it around her hair.

"You know, all the nymphs are doing this nowadays. It's a wonder you haven't caught on yet." He stepped back, furrowed his brows, and tilted his head. He held up his hands, his fingers framing Goldsprig.

"Are you done?" Goldsprig asked.

He dropped his hands and nodded.

She stood up and checked her reflection. She gasped, eyes enlarging. "I...I don't even recognize myself," she whispered.

"I'll take that as a success. My parents should be asleep. Wait for me outside while I get changed. And set up a movie in the living room while you're at it." Orchidvey smirked.

GOLDSPRING BEAT HER WINGS slowly while following behind Orchidvey. Now that they were approaching light, she could actually see what he was wearing.

He had on a sandy hoodie over a cloud gray shirt and lavender slacks. Just like her, he donned a maple cloak to cover up in the cold night air.

135

"You actually look good, Orchid."

"Thanks." Orchidvey adjusted his sandy hat and pulled out a piece of paper from his pockets to double-check the address. He stepped forward to the entrance, and motioned his friend closer.

Goldsprig looked around. Lights filled the atmosphere, while up-tempo music played distantly. Whose party was this?

"Hey, you remember me?" Orchidvey said to the bouncer at the entrance. He gestured toward Goldsprig "This is my friend here, Vesnad. She's new to town and I'm showing her around." The bouncer nodded and unlocked the gate. The two walked in and handed their cloaks to the cloakroom attendant.

Upon entering the garden, they could hear somebody gasping. "Oh my stars—Orchidvey? You're here," a voice cried out. The two turned their attention to the source and noticed a Butterfly zipping towards them. She tackled Orchidvey into a hug, almost crashing into the chairs.

"Careful, Featherjel. I'm a Flower, remember?" Orchidvey wheezed.

The Butterfly jumped off with another gasp. "I'm so sorry—I forgot." She straightened herself and placed her hands behind her back. "Who's your friend here?"

Orchidvey regained his composure. "Featherjel, meet Vesnad. Featherjel was a classmate of mine from a while back. Vesnad and I recently met."

Goldsprig smiled. "Nice to meet you."

"Hi Vesnad." Featherjel smiled back. "Any friend of Orchid is a friend of mine. Want me meet another friend?"

"Uh…" Before Goldsprig could answer, she felt Featherjel grabbing hold of her hand and dragging her away to the other side of the garden.

Featherjel led her to a karaoke machine. There was a fairy sitting in front who turned to Featherjel upon noticing her arrival.

"Hello, Featherjel. Who do you have there?" the fairy asked.

"Mallowsree, meet Vesnad. She's here with Orchid. Vesnad, this is my friend Mallowsree," said Featherjel. As if on cue, Orchidvey flew in from behind.

Goldsprig smiled and waved. Mallowsree waved back. Goldsprig eyed Mallowsree, noticing his wings were folded up like hers.

"Mallowsree, if you don't mind me asking," Goldsprig asked, "what kind of fairy are you?"

Mallowspree raised a brow, jerking his head back a bit. He cocked his head to the side for a moment before scooting out of his chair. His wings unfurled, revealing glossy aster petals pointing outward. There were yellow and a few green swirls among the dark veins, if inspected closely enough.

Mallowsree bowed. "A Flower and Dragonfly. At your service, Miss Vesnad."

"Whoa." Goldsprig gasped.

"And what about you?" Mallowsree asked.

Goldsprig swallowed. He's asking her now? She took a step back and looked over at Orchidvey, who nodded back at her with a smile.

Goldsprig blinked and turned back to Mallowsree, still waiting for an answer. She just met a biracial fairy. Someone like her. All of her life, Goldsprig never considered the fact it was possible to meet another from a mixed background like herself. Not when all she ever saw in her life were camera flashes and her vanity mirrors. She couldn't see anything beyond her celebrity persona.

Goldsprig lowered her head. But she wasn't a celebrity right now. She looked back up to Mallowsree, her eyes lingering on his wings, which he had folded up.

Why were they folded? Was it because he was embarrassed like her? Perhaps he also never met another fairy like himself, like her.

Goldsprig smiled and slowly unfurled her wings. "A Dragonfly, but also a Crystal, too."

Featherjel's jaw dropped. Mallowsree beamed, almost falling over.

"A pleasure to meet a fellow biracial individual, Miss Vesnad," said Mallowsree. He stepped forward and picked up her hand. The two smiled.

"A pleasure to you too, sir."

Goldsprig noticed Featherjel leaning over to Orchidvey and whispering something in his ear. She could feel eyes on her, a feeling she learned to recognize at a young age. A feeling she had learned to dread, something to leave her perturbed. Today, however, none of it mattered. Goldsprig straightened herself and stepped closer to Mallowsree.

"Have you ever," she asked as she pulled her hand out of his to point at her wings, "gotten stares? Fairies wanting to touch them and ask you questions?"

Mallowsree nodded. "I've gotten used to them and choose to ignore them. My wings are my business. Not theirs, Vesnad. After all, these wings are simply a reminder of my parents breaking tradition, boundaries." He waved a hand for emphasis.

Goldsprig nodded. So it was. She looked around herself. She was right about the stares, and they were coming from all directions. She stood up tall and fanned out her wings. She flapped them once, knowing they would catch the lights. There must be some sort of compathy, because Mallowscree did so too at the same moment.

"Yes, these may be different, but it's something special," she said. She stepped away from the table and into one of the many lights in the room. Her arms spread out just a bit and she could hear Orchidvey following her. "You're right," she whispered.

Goldsprig turned back around and faced Orchidvey and Mallowsree. "Yours are unique."

Mallowsree motioned back to her. "I'd argue the same about yours."

"That makes two of us. I always thought I was alone." Goldsprig smiled, eyes falling back on her wings. "Now I know I'm not."

SKY

by Diane Bui

High

Look at the clear spring sky,
Kiss your loved ones goodbye.

Clear

Look into the empyrean,
My clear eyes can see
Quiet heavens smile down at me
From old days to new, always it's blue.
My stormy eyes see
A quiet tension sneer down at me

Transitions

Sunbeams prance between
Fluffy white clouds,
Smile and wave to us from above.
A roar rumbles from a distance,
Sadly the beams are forever gone.

LOVE

by Aimee Geck

All it takes is a good heart for you to love
Beating strong; climbing the ropes;
Daring to try new things.

Even if it skews your path
Fate can change
In a matter of seconds.

Heartbeat
Inching to a stop
When you see their face.

Find time to
Love somebody.

LISTLESS STORM
by Ngoc Pham

The soft melody
Deceivingly calm, slow
When suddenly—

The tempo quickens
The rapid scales and arpeggios,
Like a gentle breeze
Turns into a blizzard

Her moment to shine is here
The four-minute piece
Practiced to perfection

So that one day he will hear
Her loneliness and anger
On her piano

WONDER

by Daniela Solano

she stands 5'7,
wide-eyed walking alone.
she watches the rain streak her glasses.
hair wet and matted,
cold squishy cheeks
from the afternoon air.
music blasting into her ears.
she runs home.
the echoing sound of loneliness surrounds her
when she makes her way into her bedroom
she watches the cold rain through the window
and draws hearts with her
cold stubby fingers.
the black buttons that were once her eyes,
now fade with the grey clouds.

its 3:30,
the world sleeps and dreams sweet.
she sits next to the same window
and counts sheep.
her mind in full daze.
the sun, being no match for the stars,
starts to rise.
alas, a new day has come.

one spring morning,
she wanders through her room.
she dances in her big t-shirt
and fuzzy pajama pants.
she makes her way through the white hallways.
pink feet warm on the cold white tiles.

she sits at the dinner table,
hearing words from last night's supper.
only today, she is alone.
a sticky note reads
"lunch in the fridge"
she plops on the couch
and feels the spring breeze
swaying her hair, making it a bigger mess.
"what are we going to do today?"
she wonders.

she spends a lot of time just doing that.
wondering.
her wondering turns to wander.
wandering in her uplifted state.

LOVE DIRECTION

by Paulvina Tran

Whether I go North,
Or head South,
Whether I look to the East,
Or watch the sun as it sets in the West,
Wherever I go,
there is your reflection,
You give me direction.
So listen carefully as I whisper this:
"If there's only four occasions,
I will be with you every Fall, Winter, Spring and Summer day.
If there's only three occasions,
I will have you in my heart **Yesterday**, **Tomorrow** and **Today**.
If there's only two occasions,
I will think of you twice, **Day** and **Night**.
And if there can be only one occasion,
I will spend a **Lifetime** holding you tight
I will love you always,
Now and **Forever"**

CHERRY BLOSSOMS

by Christina Nguyen

Cherry blossoms fall
Onto the face of the pond
On that silent night

MARIONETTE

A lonely puppet,
Sits in silence and watches
Lamenting sadness

SAVAGERY

Eyes and senses sharp;
Like a tiger in the wild,
Feasting on her prey

REWRITE THE STARS

His wish to be hers
Hoping to rewrite the stars,
Was broken, shattered

AN EMOTION IT NEVER FELT BEFORE; LOVE

by Sophia Trejo

THE COFFEE SHOP HAD its usual customers: the old couple that shared a piece of lemon meringue pie, a group of girls who were squealing over their pumpkin spice lattes, and a college student who had tiny espresso cups, notebooks and textbooks surrounding him.

In all of Noah's 224 years of existence, the sound of coffee brewing was his favorite. The sound of people screaming for their life was a close second.

As he read the newspaper in his hand, Noah slowly reached for his cup and took a sip from his piping hot coffee. The heat from it didn't bother him; he actually enjoyed the burn on the roof of his mouth.

"Mortals and their silly ideas of power." The demon thought to himself while reading an article about the president's plans for making America great again.

His eye roll was cut short due to the sound of the entrance bell ringing. Noah looked up at the door and for the first time in his existence, he felt the wind getting knocked out of *him*. In stumbled a girl. She looked like she was in her early twenties, but the overalls she worn over her pink knitted sweater made her look younger. The black, shiny boots she wore made an obnoxious squeaking sound as she walked in.

"An angel," he thought. When she took off her beanie, her brown, curly hair was pushed back by her hand as she looked up at the menu above her. Noah watched with curious eyes as she ordered her drink at the front desk. The demon was mesmerized by the way she took her wallet out of her backpack and handed the barista her credit card with a smile. He leaned forward on the table and almost knocked over his coffee cup as she went to grab some napkins from the other side of the counter.

With eyes still locked on his angel, he saw her coming towards his direction. Noah scurried back to sit normally in his seat and watched with wide eyes as she sat in the booth in front of him. The barrier of the two seats separated the demon from his angel. The demon had the urge to reach across the space to tuck a piece of the angel's hair behind her ear as she looked down to open her backpack. She pulled out a book and a pen and set them on the table in front of her. When the waiter came up to her table to set down her hot mug, the demon gripped the side of the table and scowled as the waiter gave the angel a warm smile. Noah gave him a harsh stare until he was fully behind the counter again and then softened when he looked back at the mortal.

She smiled, small and satisfied as she brought the mug to her lips. Her sweater paws held the mug to help her warm up from the bitter winter outside. Her eyes locked with his as her lips touched the rim. The demon's eyes widened and his face felt the way he burned his victims. A small gasp fell from his lips and he frantically looked away, the newspaper article on the table in front of him seeming more interesting than it did three seconds ago.

The angel took a sip from her hot drink, and with a small smile, put the mug back on the little plate. She opened up her book and clicked open her pen.

The demon's heart never felt so alive as it beat rapidly in his chest.

What is happening? Noah glared down at the table. His shaky hands brought the newspaper up to cover his heated face. Not a minute went by before he slowly brought the newspaper low enough to see her. He watched as she brought the end of her pen to her mouth, her eyebrows furrowed in concentration. As if she felt his eyes on her again, she looked up. He quickly held the newspaper back up again, cursing under his breath quietly.

"Why do I feel this way?" Noah's chest rose up and down. "A mortal, melting the heart of a demon? No. This is ridiculous." He heard rustling in front of him and panicked.

"Is she leaving?" Noah worried he might have scared her off. It's ironic isn't it? For a demon to not want to scare off a mortal; at least not in his human form anyway. Noah brought lowered his defenses and jumped in his seat when he saw her sitting at his booth, right across from him.

The angel gave him a smile and the demon swore in his 224 years of existence, that he's never seen a more beautiful sight.

THE DOG WHO COOKED

by Kayla Nguyen

Bob the corgi cooked a meal.
The ingredients sold were such a steal!
But he sang a sad song.
The pan fell down with a gong.
The burnt food was now revealed!

SPACE

by Jennifer Ho

So much around me
but I can't focus on a single thing
I stare at a blank wall,
as if it were a universe
Scribbled with words
from the fragments of my mind
My eyes unbothered,
by the movement of reality
Space is where I belong,
where my soul is finally
Free.

THE LIFE OF A DOLL

by Keanu Hua

I WAS NEVER ABLE to understand how to hold a conversation—it just seemed too tedious and chaotic. Tone, expression, connotation, body language…I just couldn't see how I was supposed to understand so many nuances in the instants that passed, yet face the consequence of never being able to fully repair them if I missed them.

So, maybe that's why I was drawn to doll making, content to sit under old elm trees during recess or break or lunch to construct another perfect creation, smiling to myself as they began to take form and eventually smile back. Whenever someone else tried to disturb the silence, all I would ever do was smile back, hoping that they'd leave, and it nearly always worked.

I was told it was a bit creepy to constantly smile like that, especially with my frail physique, looking as if I was knocking at death's door and ready to collapse at any moment. I smiled when I was adding miniscule details to my dolls that ought to have knitted my expression into one of concentration, I smiled even when brief bullies threw my dolls into the mud, and I smiled even before I fainted one warm summer day, overwhelmed by my camp's prohibition of my doll making and some other pointless factors.

Still, I returned the next day, doll-making kit in hand and a smile plastered on my pale face; I regretted my whims little, even when I saw the other kids playing with each other during free time. I figured that it would never be better than doll-making, even if others bullied me. Even then, I smiled when I ought to have grimaced.

I guess my smile was that of a doll's, sewn into my very being.

Dolls and that iconic doll-like smile were more than my everything. They never talked back, never frowned, never judged me, never hurt me, never cast me a disappointed or confused glance when I returned to talking about making a new doll as I always did—at least, never of their own free will.

Sometimes, I entertained the delusion, letting the clay or cloth contort into a foul glare, yet I found myself loving my dolls even more. But somehow, seeing the same thing in another person only made me stammer, and I would always excuse myself to leave, fearful of being tossed aside like a doll, yet I would still smile.

Like a doll.

There was only one girl that seemed to enjoy dolls just as much as me.

I was ten. It was a chilly winter day, one of those awkward days where dark clouds are only covering half of the sky, leaving the sun to shine despite the approaching oblivion. I, as always, was underneath an elm tree, smiling as I crafted a new doll: a bold looking girl with a short red comb over, her dark red jacket concealing a black shirt with a fancy little emblem. I could tell immediately that she would be a good addition to my collection, but *she* eventually disturbed me from my thoughts.

"Hi," she greeted, waving to me with a doll-like smile, "You seemed kind of lonely, so I thought I'd ask…who are you?" I took a few seconds to turn, smiling and blinking slowly as my hands continued to sew, trying to see if she wanted something. "Your name?"

I stayed silent, continuing to stare at her and hoping that she'd leave. "Come on, don't be so afraid."

"Gallo. Gallo…Dang?" I said, tilting my head. Was I supposed to say more?

"Nice to meet you. I thought you looked kind of lonely, and I'm pretty new, too. My family just moved here last week," she said with a nod. I felt my smile stretch a little more, my hands beginning to slow. "Ooh, is that a doll? I love dolls too, but I've never made one myself."

"Yes. Do you want it?" I held it out to her, the doll still incomplete and with a loose string still stuck to it, "I'm not done yet, but…"

"If you don't mind."

I nodded slowly, feeling little obligation to give it to her and turning back to my doll as my hands began to soar across its body, continuing to sew life into it, "Oh, I never gave you my name. I'm Carrie. Carrie Benson."

In the distance, a couple of seagulls cawed, and I smiled back at her. "Carrie. Sounds like a bird cawing," I said. "Carrie. Carrie." She laughed a little at that, sounding a bit like a recording or a doll, but that only made me love her more.

"My parents really wanted me to make a friend quickly," she said, her gaze turning to the birds as near silence came over both of us, the only sound my needle grazing against the fabric. "Maybe you could come to my house later today?"

I nodded, but I still faced my doll as she gave me her address. "You know, you remind me a lot of a doll. Do you think I could dress you up?" She touched my cheek, and I immediately recoiled, clutching my doll and turning away from her with a bitter expression. "Oh, sorry about that." I stared at her for a few moments, pouting as I frantically wiped away the smudge on my face. "Wow, your skin's really sensitive, huh?"

"Sorry," I muttered out, covering the lesion with my doll, "I…I…nobody's ever touched my face like that."

"Not even your parents?" I nodded.

"Not recently, no." I sighed, wiping away the last remnants with my doll. "Even a sterilized hand stains me." Yet as much as I hated the wound she had opened up, I wanted her hand in mine, her fingers to brush against me again, her warm hold to embrace me.

Like a doll. I wanted to be her doll, even if it stained me.

"Actually, I…could you maybe?" I paused.

"Yes?"

Could you touch me again?

If only I did say it.

"Never mind." I saw my parents' car, and sprang away to leave, my smile just briefly fading, but when I felt my parents' eyes back on me, my expression became a doll's again.

I could not bear to be thrown away, not this time. I was close to finding the perfect doll.

I arrived at her home later that day, a perfect little dollhouse with white walls and red roofs. Carrie was waiting at her front door, a bride ragdoll of her own and a smile sewn on her face. Immediately, I thought of trying to make a doll of her, first considering cloth, then perhaps plastic, and at least deciding on bisque porcelain.

Bisque seems right, hopefully I can sneak into dad's workshop, I thought as I walked up to her, still smiling and with my doll from earlier in my hand.

"You seem so happy all the time. Are you always smiling?" she asked as we continued through her neat house, where there was not one misplaced object.

"Yes," I said as we opened the door to her room, giving her a mechanical tilt of my head, "Dolls smile all the time. Why shouldn't I?"

"Fair enough," she said with a chuckle. Carrie walked over to a walk-in closet with a mirror, opening it and tossing her bride doll into my hands. "Now then, I need to find the outfit I picked out for you."

"Why do you want to dress me up, anyway?"

"When I saw you earlier…I don't know why, but I just really wanted to. I guess it's because you look a lot like a doll."

I nodded as my smile became a beaming grin, pleased that she thought well of me.

Eventually she opened the closet and gestured towards the outfit she had prepared for me. "My dad gave this to me. He's a costume designer."

151

I first noticed the light gray cloak, which had pink and orange flowers and patterns on the sides that would have been sealed up if it was a proper jacket, alongside a series of ridges on its open sides, perhaps where buttons would have been, but it lacked any.

Before she could say anything, I walked towards it, grabbed it, and put it on, feeling its colds, almost plastic-like material envelop me, and as I inspected myself in the mirror door, I found that it did quite match me.

Next, she gave me similarly-colored peaked cap, one that reminded me of some Asian police officer in a movie I saw once. As I put it on, our smiles widened.

"Hmm, I think the rest of this will need you to ch—"

"No, I don't want to."

"What? Come on, it'll be fun. You don't have to worry; I won't even look. Look at how good you already look with just those. Here, let me show you the rest of the outfit." She slid out the next parts from their coat hangers—two sashes, one turquoise and the other orange and pink floral-print, for my waist, black shorts rimmed in an ashen grey, a pair of black gaiters with red ribbons, and a black long-sleeved shirt with pairs of buttons connected by strings on a cream yellow pillar in the center of it.

"You..." I looked away from her as I thought. You are my doll.

"I can't do it."

"Oh, that's too bad." She turned away from her closet for a moment. "Oh, wait, I have my own, too. It's not fun when it's only you dressing up." She reached into her closet, taking out a brilliantly bright bridal outfit, which I instinctively touched. "Hmm?"

"I don't know." I continued to touch it, feeling its soft white fabric in my hand, watching the way its yellow fabric fluttered softly as I brushed it, and listening to the rustle of the blue sash as it flew in the gentle breeze blowing through her room. "I don't know."

She simply watched as I felt the dress, but I could intuit that I had fallen into her trap. Rather than give up, she had decided to use the easiest way to dig me out of my shyness. Through taking out her dress, she became my doll, and I would have to join her.

"I guess I'll do it, since you will," I said.

"Great." She shoved my outfit into my hands and rushed off to another room to change. "Don't worry. I'll knock on the door first."

It wasn't long before both of us were done, and when Carrie opened the door, I somehow smiled more, noticing a subtle curiosity in her eyes as to how I could possibly grin more.

152

Nonetheless, it vanished, and she took a black camera from on top of her nightstand. "My mom's. She takes pictures for my dad's shows. Now come on, let me take a picture of you. You're such a perfect doll."

As the camera snapped the picture, I felt that something went wrong. Initially, I thought that maybe my doll smile contorted into a little grimace, my doll eyes opened a little too wide, my doll skin seemed a little uncannily familiar, but what was for sure was that something went wrong, and I felt my smile disintegrate as I noticed Carrie's worried expression.

"Ah, hold on, let me try to do that again," she said.

I snuck up on her and glanced at the preview within the camera.

For a few moments, I saw nothing wrong, but I eventually noticed my expression, or rather, the lack thereof. It was like looking at a completely blank white mask whose face was just almost-human but not quite.

I didn't mind most human-like dolls, but the mask that had somehow fallen over my face in the photograph was nothing that I had ever seen before. It was a mask trying desperately to be human, a doll trying desperately to be real, a child trying desperately to understand their parents, only to fail just a little bit and be a grim reminder of something that had never existed in full until too distant in the future.

I was thankful for the distance between me and Carrie's camera—I felt that if I tried to look at it any closer, it would sew into me an unforgettable memory, but I could tell it was hewn from my own memories, and I felt like a broken doll of iron threads, paralyzed rather than mobile, and freezing cold rather than warming, yet never to be repaired because of how fearful it was to gaze upon my injured doll body.

It was not a past I had ever shared, even to my foster family, yet as the mask in the photo gazed back with the cold, forgotten eyes of an abandoned doll, I could not help but wonder. A familiar stare, one I had once embodied in the past.

My stare. The one I regarded everyone with, doll like and false, and a layer of falsehood that would tear me apart to save others. My mind began to swirl.

How long ago was it when I had to be given up for a better life, when my now long-forgotten home lost its name and my parents decided that this was not the life for me, and so traded me like a newly-made doll of a peasant to some noble's household?

How long ago was it when I last heard their piercing cries as I glimpsed them with petrified doll-like eyes for the last time, giving them a silly promise that I would still not become an object, a plaything, a doll as well? I could not recall the time and date, but I did not wish to.

Not with Carrie, and not for her; the promise had been vacuous anyway.

153

"Delete it," I said.

"What?"

"I said delete it. Delete it. Delete it. Delete it. Delete. It." A few pop-ups later, and it vanished, leaving us two dolls in silence. "Sorry about that," I said. "I don't norm—"

"It's okay, Gallo. It'll be okay." She patted my shoulder, but I did not recoil. "Hmm? You're not…"

I closed my eyes, letting my smile return as I walked away from her, feeling her soft fingers trail against my back before I eventually turned around. "Come on, take my picture."

"Really? After what just—"

"Yes, really."

There was a click, and she smiled as she looked at the preview, yet I could detect a hint of regret for her earlier words. Doll was an apt description for me, but I could never let anyone know why I hated to be one, why I despised the fiber of my being yet found it a duty to allow others to love it.

I realized that, whatever I chose to be, I was fated to fail someone. What would my parents think when they realized that their son broke his promise? What would everyone else think when they realized that the dutiful boy they knew was a fraud, motivated not by altruism, but by a desperation to survive?

What would Carrie think?

Her voice caught my attention. "Hold on, let me get a picture of both of us." She put the camera on the nightstand, set a timer on it, and rushed towards me. "Cheese."

I glanced at her, noticing her completely perfect smile, not sewn in like a doll's, but natural, like a person's. She did not smile for the doll's duty, but smiled for love.

After a short while, another click, followed by her grabbing her camera and showing me the preview. "See? Isn't it just per—great? I'll give you a copy tomorrow, okay? I'll have my mom clean it up so we can both use it."

I nodded.

"Do you think you could take my picture too?" she asked.

I did and soon enough we were both looking at yet another picture.

"Mmm, that's great, too," she said.

One last nod.

The rest of the day blitzed by, and before either of us knew it, I had to leave with an almost curt, "Farewell," but it was hard to let her go like that, especially with the subtle twinge of regret that paralyzed me as I stepped into my parents' car.

"Honey, you okay?" my foster mother's voice called out.

"Goodbye, Carrie," I blurted out, watching her smile grow just a little more as I finally closed the door.

It was still not enough for either of us, though—she persisted on the steps of her house and I rolled down the window to look at her without the darkened windows, the two of us continuing to give each other doll-like smiles until long out of sight.

"Made a friend, huh?" my mother asked as we drove back, a hint of relief in her voice.

"Yes, I did. She loves dolls, too. She dressed me up and we both pretended to be dolls."

"Oh, that's really nice."

Time flew by, and my visits to Carrie's became a near-weekly occurrence. At first, it was mostly dressing each other up, but as we got older we found it better to just talk, bemoan our current assignments, help each other, and only after all that would the two of us work on doll making.

Though her hands were initially clumsy, she refused to give up as I helped her make her own dolls, and though she always insisted that they were never as good as mine, I always reassured her and told her that every doll had to be imperfect to be human.

Eventually, she complained that her hands hurt when she was helping me, and so I returned to my craft once more alone, with only the eyes of others to accompany me.

Every day, though, we would start with the same conversation. "Carrie?"
"Yeah?"

Do you want to try again? I know it's hard, but trust me, you'll love it
"Maybe...do you want to...never mind."

Curse my reluctance. Why was it so hard to say it, but so easy to regret it?

But still, as I spent time with her, I began to wonder what it would have been like if I had been more inviting to those that had dared to wander near me.

The other kids always thought I was a bit weird, but sometimes the smarter or more social or kinder of them would walk near me, try to start up a conversation, and leave when I flashed them my infamous doll smile.

As I later found out, Carrie was all three, but as successful as she was, she never really found love, even all the way through high school, even when so many of the other boys—some of whom were remarkably charming, others foolishly attempting a dare—tried to catch her.

She would always return to my side, and the two of us would leave, me with a doll in hand. I remained interested in doll making throughout school, even as it earned me the relentless bullying of my classmates.

That, I could bear.

What I could hardly bear were the thoughts of friendship that became whispers of love, words of romance, and eventually hands of hateful jealousy. One day during my freshman year, I had been rounding a corner at my high school when I suddenly heard shouting.

"I don't get it, why are you interested in some creep like him? All he does is smile and make those...weird dolls. How do you know he isn't planning on turning you into one?"

"Excuse me? He's way more interesting than you think. Just because he's not like most of us doesn't mean that he doesn't deserve someone that'll care for him," Carrie said. "Just because he's not from here doesn't mean that he has to be mistreated. He's nicer than you, at least."

I felt my smile, my whole face even, begin to crack as I listened to the argument.

"Of course he's not from here. With how pale he is, he's probably just some robot that you accidentally fell in love with. It's a wonder how something like him can function."

"Accidentally? It was never. It had been our choices to begin with."

"A bad choice on your part, then. Come on, Carrie, you deserve someone bet—"

"I'm not falling for that disgusting lie again. I've heard all about you from everyone else. You're nothing like the lady killer you think you are."

She picked up her bags and left, thankfully in the opposite direction, but I eventually heard a grunt of surprise when she fell to the floor, followed by sadistic chortling. It ended there, with all three of us dispersing.

When I visited Carrie later that day, I could tell she had been crying.

"Not now, Gallo," she said.

"I'm sorry, Carrie."

"Hmm? What for?"

"For earlier."

"You were there? Why didn't you help me?"

"Because I...I heard about it from a friend, it's—I wasn't there."

"Gallo, you're lying."

"I'm sorry, Carrie," I clutched the doll in my hands harder, "I did—"

"They were right, weren't they?" she said.

I felt the stuffing of my doll begin to squeeze out onto my hand.

She looked away. "You really are just some dumb robot."

The doll exploded in my hands into a storm of stuffing, and as I looked down I felt as though I was looking upon a murder scene, "No. No, no, no, no, no, no, no!"

"See? You really do sound like some broken record now!"

"Carrie…"

I love you.

"I'm sorry." I ran off, ignoring the stuffing coating me as I sobbed back to my house.

The next day, the boy that had bullied her was victim to a bisque doll shattering on his head, an incomplete one that was supposed to be Carrie that I had spent the last five years perfecting and that I no longer deemed sacred like the rest of my collection.

I was suspended for five days, but even worse lost my doll-making privileges for the day after. When I returned, everyone was suddenly afraid of me again.

Everyone except Carrie.

"I'm sorry for what I said, Gallo."

"It's okay. I'm…really such an idiot. I should've—"

"Shh." She put her finger on my lips and stained my skin. "It'll be okay, Gallo. He didn't know what he was saying either, and…I can see why you did that. Thank you."

She brushed my cheek, and I closed my eyes as I felt her unfamiliar warmth on my cold porcelain, feeling its flame of love temper and glaze it. As she drew away, I felt as though she had just painted my face, as though I was her porcelain doll.

"Carrie…"

I love you.

"Thank you," I said, pausing as regret bubbled within me for failing to be honest, "Thank you for everything. And I'm sorry I wasn't bra—"

"I can tell you had to be brave just to talk to me when we first met, and that's enough."

The year blitzed by, and soon enough, everyone was beginning to plan for prom.

"Hey, Gallo," Carrie began, watching as I shaped the clay for a new bisque doll, "I was thinking…do you want to be my prom king?"

"No. No. No," I replied, for once taking my eyes off of my doll and looking back at her, "Nobody likes me, you know that. I won't get any votes."

"I'll try, I always can and always do," she reassured me, but I could tell it would ruin her chances at prom queen.

157

"You really shouldn't, you really shouldn't. Just…be prom queen, without me. That's fine, right?"

"G-Gallo." She paused. I had never heard her stammer before. "I don't care what they think. I just want to be with you."

I stared back at her, not sure what to say, and eventually returned to working, incredulous to her implications, but I heard a small voice whisper within my mind.

I love you.

But I've learned my reluctance was because I couldn't believe my own heart, and not a day goes by that I don't regret saying something, saying anything, saying that yes, I wanted to be with her, yes, society will be at the side, yes, she is my one and only doll.

And yet I did not.

In the end, she forced me in anyway, and I found myself thankful that she did.

The two of us adorned the school in posters and with dolls that a surprising many of students found adorable, but it still was not enough to wipe away the fact I smashed a bisque doll over someone's head, and her votes fell with mine. Instead, two other popular no-names rose to prom queen and king.

Carrie and I, though, were content to our obscurity and hundreds of dolls.

It did not last, though: June came with tragedy.

"Gallo, what university are you going to?"

"Citrine University, why?" She grimaced. "Is something the problem?"

"Yes, it is. I have to go to Achlys-Tapputi," she said, "Geez, I guess that means this is going to be our last month together, huh?"

I love you.

The words refused to utter from my throat.

I love you.

I could not, for I was a doll and meant to only be loved, so I could not possibly fall in love with my owner. Yet why did I feel its tug nonetheless?

I love you.

It was what I should have said, but I stayed silent.

As much as I tried to savor my last moments with her, they escaped from my limp doll grasp with ease. Days turned to minutes, weeks were but hours, and the month went by like a second, and all the while I felt like a doll being crushed.

Time flew by, my hands grew less and less steady, my focus less and less able, and my love more and more painful.

At school, my classmates and even Carrie assumed it to be part of the "senioritis" plague going around, and gave my forced smile no further thought or complaint.

158

Sometimes, when I figured nobody was looking, I would let it slacken, finding it unbearable to continue to pretend like that. Then, I would force my smile back on, hoping that nobody would notice my reddened pale eyes that had spent hours crying for my love.

Our last day together was our last summer.

"So, guess this is really our last day together, huh?" she asked as we sat underneath another elm tree in the park, watching our classmates' final senior celebration in the distance, "Tomorrow, a plane to Achlys-Tapputi."

"Yes," I said, nearly choking again as she let her head lean against my shoulder; but even these simple gestures and phrases were tearing at my heart, "Carrie…do you regret anything?"

"No, not really. I think I could die happy," she snuggled against me, curling up like a person while I left my own body sprawled out against the tree like a doll that was tossed aside, "You do know how I feel, right?"

I nodded and began to sob as I felt the fulmination of my love detonate within me, as I felt my doll heart shatter. As I suddenly felt, for once, that I could be human, that I had something within my hollow crevice of a chest, and that I did not have to pretend to be a doll.

"What's wrong, Gallo? Why are you crying?" she asked, continuing to hold onto me as I sprang up. "Please don't cry."

"It's nothing," I said, overwhelmed by the pain, "It's nothing, Carrie."

But I love you.

As I gazed on her through the tears, I felt that this was not meant to be, that telling her that I loved her, that I would be her doll, that I was human because of her, would only bring her more pain. So, I began to run away, but she held onto my arm, refusing to let me go.

"You're acting…not like yourself, Gallo," she said, freezing me in place.

"Carrie, let go."

"I won't let go, not until you tell me why you're acting so different."

"Different?" I turned to her, brimming with anger and not caring what I said if it would finally let her leave unburdened, "That's what everyone says, and now you too. Carrie, we both know that I was never like anyone, and I never could be. I don't understand why you loved me. Just forget about me, Carrie."

But I still love you.

She let me go, and I fled home. When I looked back, I could tell that she too was beginning to cry.

Later that night, she called me to apologize, but I refused to respond, thinking that starting a conversation would inevitably lead me to confessing and more tears and more heartbreak and more pain for her. As much as it pained me to have to deal with my newfound heart alone, I refused to let Carrie handle the burden too, and so I lied in bed alone, desiring the warmth of another to accompany the new warmth burning within me.

The next day, I found her completed bisque doll in my dad's workshop, which I took and cradled in my arms, wondering what it would be like if maybe I had said something, if maybe I was wrong. So, with a sudden whim, I began to walk to her house, carrying her doll in my hand.

I got there just as she was loading her things into her parents' car. "Carrie," I called out, feeling new energy surge within me and feeling a strange wholeness just being near her.

"Gallo, you should've said you'd come to see me leave." She sighed. "I'm sorry about everything that happened la—"

"Here. Take it," I said, shoving the doll towards her, finding it a little odd that I was smiling a genuine, human smile rather than that of a dutiful doll. "And I'm sorry, too."

"It's fine, Gallo. But I really can't take it along since I have to go by plane." I continued to smile, finding it impossible not to with her near me. "Actually, no. I'll take it along. I'm sure I'll figure out a way to carry it into my dorm."

"That's great, Carrie, that's great." I nodded.

And I love you.

"Guess this really is our last goodbye," she said, "but one last thing..."

"Yes?"

She kissed me, and I felt my doll face revive with vibrant color.

I love you too.

"Goodbye, Carrie," I simply said.

"Goodbye, Gallo."

I walked back home, at which point I collapsed on my bed, completely exhausted, but most of all filled with regret, filled with the phrase "I love you" repeated one after the other, filled with futures now gone.

And I knew I would never get my chance—the world was much too wide, and though I fancied my wishes of love to be far reaching, I knew it would be a stretch to think that one letter or one doll would be enough to find her again.

But still, I wait.

Sometimes, I see her in my dreams or in my dolls, a specter of my past that would vanish as soon as it came, and I would either wake up or simply stare, unsure of what to do, but paralyzed by her grim reminder. When I saw it, I would become aware once more of my human heartbeat, and how each rumble it made was another rumble of regret.

Yet to feel her again, even in that painful way, was simple euphoria for me, and each heartbeat brought bittersweet joy to me.

Eventually, I would feel it fade, and for a short while I would sob, wishing again for another rush of love to remind me that I was not a doll.

But, that is The Life of A Doll, wishing to be human and only being loved, and when we love, it only makes our inevitable discarding all the worse. Yet I know that the best of dolls would be the ones that can love and reciprocate, that will say "I love you" out of their own will rather than as a recording.

If only I was like that.

LIKING SOMEONE IS WEIRD

by Jessica Lai

You see *them*
your jaw drops at their effortless beauty
their smile brings you joy—
the reason your day brightens on the gloomiest of days.
liking someone is weird.
In your world,
more than anyone else,
they make you the happiest.
But they might not feel the same way
and that hurts.
Even if you want them more
than the depths of the earth,
they may want someone else.
Luck seems to determine your happy ending.
And liking someone is liking more
than the front cover of their book
Liking someone is seeing all
the little things they do
Every scroll, every flip of a page,
every word

Reminds you of the smell of their thick jacket
or the thinnest of shirts
Your heart dances
And then, possibly, your romantic dreams
become a reality,
Or not.
So what? Go on, live your best life

because somewhere, out there, amongst us,
Someone cares.
Even if it's not the someone
You thought you liked.
Man…
liking someone is really weird.

OBLIVISCATUR
by Kelly Ho

I watch as your shadow fades
Into the light. You disappear.
The world shatters, yet I smile.

Waiting like a Pierrot,
Holding back my tears,
Missing the pieces of you.

In the place you'll never return,
Your remnants remain like *déjà vu*.
Wanting to forget but I never can.

Rewind the time to when it was us.
Even if in you now I don't exist,
At least in these memories we remain.

Images that stain my mind,
I'll let them continue to paint me
With the colors that you've long forgotten.

Our ending, your goodbye
Everything will fade away.
Our remnants become *déjà vu*.

Close my eyes, let myself sink in,
Forget about the reality of us.
Our love remains at least in me.

SUNFLOWER

by Iris Sanchez

Her image lingers in my head
She stole my heart completely
She makes me wonder, makes me worry
"How much longer will you stay?"
She never faces my way, but always smiling bright
She's a sunflower
Oh, she's *my* sunflower
Blooming in December weather
growing in a garden full of roses
She stands tall, proudly boasting her colors
Yet shows insecurity when light retreats
Always reaching for the sun, this wonderful flower.
How much longer can I help you grow?
How much more time will we have together?
Sunflower, my beautiful sunflower
Please keep growing, even without me by your side.

A PARENT'S SACRIFICE

by Nancy Huynh

The day I came to the United States
And traded my parents' dreams for mine
I felt the pressure, buried from the weight
Of future tasks assigned to heirs in line

My mother was an angel to her peers,
My father was the one loved by the town
But when they came with luggage filled with tears
The language border took away their crown

I strive to replace the souls my parents lost
To take the throne and lead this era's reign
To repay all their efforts and their costs
The blood and sweat they shed are not in vain

Away from home, endeavor overseas
A parent's sacrifice, the key to be me

SEASONS

by Vivian Tang

--Spring

I stood in front of you.
Flowers clenched tightly in my hands.
I did my best to avoid your gaze,
your soft and mesmerizing gaze.
Never dared to look into your eyes.
But you did it again.
You stepped back
further away,
opening space between us.
Before I knew it, you were
speaking the words
I never wished to hear.

*How many times
have I told you not to do this?*

Your facial expression unreadable
a poker face as your façade.
My hands shook uncontrollably;
beads of perspiration cascaded down my face.
But my reply was always the same.

Why won't you accept it?

I tried to sound brave
but hiding behind a mask of bravery,
it only took another sentence
for you to break me.

There's no reason for me to.

167

Your voice cold as ice
even on this warm spring day.
I wanted to say something else,
you were already gone,
leaving behind a blank space
where you used to be.
I closed my eyes, wincing at the sharp stings
before my eyes poured heavy rain.
You left before I could say anything.
I wanted to give you pansies.

--*Summer*

Look at the sun shining,
trying to mimic you,
but it stood no chance.
As if the sun can only frown,
your beauty can't be replicated.
My heart raced.
Your smile so vibrant
I swear, even fireworks
can't melt me like you do.
You shook your head to sweep your bangs aside
while you laughed wholeheartedly.
Even the way you laughed was pure.
I wondered to myself,
how did God create such a perfect human
when no one else in this world was perfect?
But as the ringing in my ears subsided,
I bit my lips tightly.
I was going to do this again and again.
My persistent mind told me to continue on
no matter how many times I got rejected.
Because I only have this life to tell you.

The same scene repeats.
You stood in front of me
with your unreadable expression
as I hung my head low,

extending the flower out
toward you nonetheless.

Aren't you tired?

I don't get tired of seeing your face,
and certainly, don't get tired of seeing you.
But again, no words came out of my mouth.
I muted myself with my anxiety,
and silence surrounded the two of us.

Are you doing this
because you want my money?

You spoke up, harsher than that summer's heat.
I shook my head furiously in response.

I would never do that.

Money strewed the floor.
I lifted my head to ask you why,
but the only thing I saw was
how you walked away so cruelly
without ever turning back.
I wanted to give you asters.

--Autumn

You were alone in the art room, painting.
I hid the flowers behind my back
and stepped closer to look at your canvas.
I saw red and gold leaves.

Why are you here?

I realized that we were closely connected by Autumn.
I was the falling leaf, falling deeply for you
but you were the tree that shed me.
    It's beautiful.

I loved it as much as I loved you.
You seemed taken aback
with muffled words that I couldn't hear,
but I found you so adorable
that I wished my eyes were cameras
to capture this moment
and keep it forever.

Extended my hands in front of you,
I held onto the flowers tightly,
again looking down.
Afraid of rejection but still wanting to try
to test my limits.
I found myself surprised that
I came this far.

Please, stop doing this.

And when I looked up,
you were gone, but your painting?

Still there.

I admired every little detail on the canvas.
Like the autumn sky, it was empty between us.
The smell of musk shrouding the room
still lingered some of your sweetness,
the gentle human that I once knew.
I wanted to give you primroses.

--*Winter*

I breathed out shakily,
the cold air freezing.
Rubbing my fists together,
gorses bloomed from the warmth.
I took a deep breath and knocked on the door.
Within seconds, you were there,
standing in front of me

dressed in your pajamas,
your eyes still had hints of sleep.
You looked so cute,
a blush colored my cheeks.
My heart accelerated.
The urge to wrap you into my embrace grew.
But I knew I couldn't.

Are you an idiot?

It was the first time
I heard you scream like that.
Taken aback by the sudden thunder of words,
my heart raced faster,
not from Love but from Fear.
I looked at you.
I finally looked into your eyes for the first time.

Maybe I am one.

Cut it out. Why are you so persistent?
I've rejected you countless times.
A normal person would've given up at this point.
Why are you still doing this?

The answer was simple,
but I shouldn't tell you.
Because you just wouldn't understand.
So this time, it was my turn to leave.

For the first and last time.

A Happy Poem

by Hiep Do
(Dedicated to my friend Aysha)

I'm not going to tell myself to laugh
Because it's okay to cry sometimes.
When I try to fake a laugh
Tears can't stop falling from my eyes.

Life to me feels like quicksand
Holding onto my feet
As I watch you walk away
I try to call out to you
But my voice silenced
By the sound of you walking away.

I feel myself slowly sinking
Suffocating
with the thoughts of losing you
I wish you would just turn around
And watch me as I sink
I wish you would come running back
To ask if I'm okay
Yet it all feels like a dream
As the quicksand drags me down

I wish you knew how far I ran
To be able to see your smile again
I feel like I have crossed
the entire universe
Just to get to where you are
Still, I'm a few thousand miles short
From where I am
to your heart.

If by any chance you find this poem
Don't cry when you read it
No matter how much hurting it has caused
You see, this is a happy poem
So if you smile when you read it
Maybe somewhere, near or far
I'll smile, too.

AUTHOR BIOS

Diane Bui

Hailing from the city of Fountain Valley, Diane Bui discovered the power of writing at a young age. As she grew, so did her imagination and writing skills. Armed with ideas old and new, Diane strives to design a world where anything can happen... in a book, of course.

Andy Cu

Originally from Southern California, Andy Cu grew up with a love for computers and memes. He likes to write as a hobby and hopes to share his pieces with others with the publication of "The Hunt."

Hiep Do

Born and raised in Vietnam, Hiep Do has now lived in the United States for seven years. He enjoys reading and writing whenever he has the time. Although he has written a few short stories, he especially enjoys writing poems. He hopes to major in English Literature and become a great teacher.

Aimee Geck

Aimee Geck grew up going to the beach and spending her days in the sun. She developed a love for reading at a young age and later that love blossomed into creativity which led her to pursue photography and writing. You can follow her @aimeegraphy on Instagram.

Jennifer Ho

Born in California, Jennifer T. Ho is an aspiring journalist who cares about the environment and its animals. Her favorite genre of writing is poetry and her favorite color is red. She also goes by the nickname "Yennifer" and likes photography and gaming.

Kelly Ho
Born in California, Kelly Ho grew up surrounded by many supportive family members who encouraged her to learn. Although she developed a love for reading later than her peers, her interest led her to delve into the world of writing. As college approaches, Kelly dreams of going into the medical field.

Michelle Hoang
Born in Garden Grove, California, Michelle Hoang has always loved to write. As a young child, she kept a journal of her stories and thoughts. She also expresses her creativity through her love of piano. Outgoing and playful, Michelle enjoys playing soccer on her high school team.

Keanu Hua
Often lost in his imagination, Keanu Hua relished every creative writing opportunity in elementary, but did not begin writing outside of school until seventh grade. His story "The Life of a Doll" is based on some of his characters' obsessions over dolls and their struggle for love.

Nancy Huynh
Originally from Vietnam, Nancy Huynh grew up in Westminster where she became a music fanatic and self-proclaimed boba queen. She finds joy in learning new languages, exploring different cities, and writing poetry. Her supportive family inspires her to be lighthearted and optimistic.

Jessica Lai
Short in stature, Jessica Lai grew up in California. She tends to laugh at dumb things, and text or call her online friends. She plays games and aspires to be a YouTuber. Jessica started writing last year and enjoys writing about her thoughts and feelings.

Michelle Lam
Born in California, Michelle Lam is a Vietnamese-American who prefers to spend her time bringing stories to life through sketching and writing. Although now in high school, she still collects plushies, unicorn figurines, and dolls. She strives to one day inspire dreams in children's lives.

Tiffany Le
Born in Fountain Valley and raised in Santa Ana, Tiffany Le later moved to Westminster where her love for art was reinvigorated and her love for video games and all things geeky was found. When she has free time, she likes to jot down ideas for stories and comics.

Bethanie Luu
Originally from California, Bethanie Luu grew up in Fountain Valley with a love for ice skating, literature, and writing, but she hid away her stories until now. With the publication of her poems "Hiroshima" and "Alone," she hopes to inspire others.

Vy Ngo
Vy Ngo was born in January in the Ben Tre province of southern Vietnam. She immigrated to California in 2010 and during school she discovered a love for history and English, and shortly thereafter...creative writing.

Christina Nguyen
Raised in Bakersfield, Christina Nguyen lives in Westminster where she has discovered her love for writing, badminton, and boba. She yearns to see snow again and to improve her creative writing skills. Currently, she can be seen daydreaming or roaming the campus of La Quinta with her colorful variety of plushies.

Jacqueline Duyen Nguyen
Originally from California, Jacqueline Nguyen grew up in Westminster where she developed a passion for volleyball and has been playing since 2014. Aside from volleyball, she has a love for boba, and her favorite subject is history. Jacqueline aspires to be a therapist in the future and hopes to get accepted into UCLA.

Kayla Nguyen
From California, Kayla Nguyen grew up in Westminster where she found a love for reading, puppies and, of course, writing. Although she has written since a young age, Kayla took her writing more serious within the last year. She hopes to one day travel to another part of the world.

Valerie Nguyen
Valerie Nguyen from Fountain Valley grew up with an interest in writing fictional stories and volunteering. She enjoys traveling and aspires to become a social worker and a published author. Her hope is to help others through her writing.

Aysha Pena
Born in Southern California, Aysha Pena was raised in Westminster, Orange County where she developed a passion for writing, music, and art. Her creativity is mostly expressed through poetic tunes on a piece of paper. In the future, Aysha hopes to be a recognizable American poet, artist, and writer.

Kathy Pham
Kathy Pham, born and raised in Garden Grove, California, grew up to enjoy various forms of art, such as painting and crafting. From a young age, Kathy has always had a fascination with fairy tales and fantasy novels. Her first published poem is "A Tragedy In Four Parts."

Ngoc Pham
Having immigrated from Vietnam to America at the age of eight, Ngoc grew up in Westminster where she discovered a love for TV shows, superheroes, and reading. Because of her interest in traveling, she hopes in the future to see beautiful places around the world.

Krista Phanpraphou
Channeling her Khmer bloodline, Krista Phanpraphou expresses her jokester nature through cringey poems. With her daily dose of Vietnamese coffee, she's determined to become a future veterinarian and finish her education. Despite her 4'11 height, she waddles across the track field in hopes of achieving her summer body.

Iris Sanchez
Born in California, Iris Sanchez grew up in Santa Ana where she discovered drawing, writing and music. You can find doodles and poems on her homework assignments. Iris aspires to go to college and travel the world.

Daniela Solano
Born in California into a reserved household, Daniela Solano enjoys expressing herself through her various passions, which include writing, music, and dancing. She one day hopes to be an inspiration for people who feel trapped within the constraints of society/family, unable to convey their creativity.

Vivian Tang
Born and raised in California, Vivian Tang learned to value education and self-expression through writing. As a unique and charismatic teenager, Vivian befriends everyone with her bubbly personality and contagious laughter. She is passionate about watercolor painting, tear-jerking dramas, and to launch her career in the medical field.

Phuong Traceyle
Originally from Garden Grove, Phuong Traceyle lives in Westminster. She is energetic, funny, and kind to her friends and family. She loves boba and playing sports with her cousins. Her first published works include her poem "Seasons" and her short story "The Final Battle" in the anthology *Out of Ink*.

Paulvina Tran
Born in November in California, Paulvina Tran grew up in Santa Ana trying to discover her talents. She has a wild imagination, loves writing stories, and likes to sing.

Sophia Trejo
Sophia Trejo was born in Garden Grove and has always loved to read. Her spark for writing started out as a side hobby that quickly lead to her passion. Trejo's dream is to one day see her name in The New York Times as a best-selling author.

Jacqueline Truong
Jacqueline Truong is an aspiring artist but more so an aspiring writer, having found her passion for writing in first grade. Though mostly an author of fiction, poetry has been growing on her and "Lacrimosa" is her first published poem.

Christine Vu
Despite her clumsiness, Christine Vu smiles often even while bumping into objects. In addition to writing, she enjoys listening to European music and prides herself on her ice-cream sundaes. She hopes to one day travel around Europe and work in the filming industry.

www.ingramcontent.com/pod-product-compliance
Lightning Source LLC
Chambersburg PA
CBHW070030260626
47159CB00005B/1998